BULLET JUSTICE

To some, Walt Slade is a fearless and capable Texas Ranger, diligent in his enforcement of the law. Others know him only by his undercover identity, *El Halcón* — The Hawk — the fastest gunhand in the whole Southwest, who pursues justice for the oppressed. In the booming oil town of Echo, Slade is called in to help deal with a shrewd and ruthless outlaw bunch causing trouble. Stagecoaches, stores, and saloons have been robbed at gunpoint — and someone tries to shoot Slade before he even sets foot in the town. Meanwhile, Jaggers Dunn, general manager of the C. & P. Railroad System, has ambitious plans to extend the network into the surrounding land. The townsfolk approve of the railroad development, hoping it will enhance Echo's prosperity. But then someone attempts to blow up a locomotive engine in a seemingly senseless attack . . .

BULLET JUSTICE

BRADFORD SCOTT

SAGEBRUSH
Large Print Westerns

First published in the United States by Pyramid Books

First Isis Edition
published 2018
by arrangement with
Golden West Literary Agency

A catalogue record for this book is available
from the British Library.

ISBN 978–1–78541–555–5 (pb)

Published by
F. A. Thorpe (Publishing)
Anstey, Leicestershire

Set by Words & Graphics Ltd.
Anstey, Leicestershire
Printed and bound in Great Britain by
T. J. International Ltd., Padstow, Cornwall

This book is printed on acid-free paper

CHAPTER
ONE

A tarnished gem in a lavish setting of green and gold, the oil town of Echo hunkered in the Texas hills on the bottom of a great bowl torn by some terrific convulsion of Nature.

The basin was very old. A million years and more had passed since it came into being to the accompaniment of fire spouting volcanoes and thundering tidal waves. And during those eons of time, many things had happened to the bowl and its area.

Foremost, from mankind's point of view, was the slow but steady seepage from a vast oil pool to the north that, because of the great depth of its setting and the lack of adequate machinery, man had so far been unable to tap. But a depression under the bowl had received the seepage oil and stored it up to ultimately be exploited by the wildcat driller who had a nose for petroleum and sniffed it out.

But the great pool to the north was untouched so far, and on the rangeland to the north, the cow was still supreme, the cattleman still king.

Very few wildcatters even suspected the great pool to the north, and if they had, it would not have interested them. They were content to exploit the not-small pool

1

under the basin. So on the bottom of the basin stood a veritable forest of drilling derricks, with the town of Echo shouldering against them.

And at the moment, Echo was thinking of things other than what was responsible for its inception: oil; of something that might well greatly enhance its prosperity and perhaps enable it to attain a permanent status as a city independent of oil for its existence, that could continue to flourish after the oil pool under the basin was drained.

Twenty miles to the south was Tumble, the other oil town of the section, opened before Echo. Better than thirty miles to the southwest was Sanderson, the railroad town, a crew change point for the great East-West line, with extensive shops and yards.

A short line connected with the East-West line south of Tumble and ran north to Tumble, hence to Echo — the line to Echo recently completed — and entered the town by way of a breakthrough piercing the south slope of the Echo bowl. Formerly, the only way to reach Echo was by an old, very old, trail that zig-zagged up the south slope, across its crest and down the opposite sag to the floor of the bowl.

Now, however, there was plenty of room for a horse cart, paralleling the right of way. Which facilitated cart trains bearing casings and other badly needed materials.

Formerly, the broad crest had been brush-grown, but a fire set by outlaws had scorched and cleaned out most of the brush, temporarily, and came unpleasantly close to cleaning out the town.

2

Now the growth was coming back, tall and thick and green.

The hills surrounding the basin were low, comparatively speaking, but rugged. The railroad continued straight across the basin to the northern slope, through which a cut, almost completed, would break through. Already the main line and a couple of long sidings almost stretched to the breakthrough, piercing the northern slope. The breakthrough had been delayed by weather conditions and a shortage of vital materials. But now only a few lengths of track were needed to drive the steel through the base of the slope and onto the rangeland to the north, where shops and a big assembly yard were under construction.

For James G. "Jaggers" Dunn, the general manager and moving force of the great C. & P. Railroad System, planned a line to tap the rich farming lands to the north and west of the Winter Gardens and not far from Fort Stockton, which had never been fully developed because of the lack of adequate transportation facilities; and from there west by south to Alpine and link with the East-West line, tapping the mining properties on the way, which also badly needed better transportation facilities. An ambitious program that was expected to do great things for Echo.

So Echo was humming, and would hum louder tomorrow, decidedly so, for tomorrow the formal breakthrough would be accomplished, with the general manager himself expected to be present for the ceremony.

And, astride a magnificent black horse, riding from Sanderson, was the man Dunn hoped most of all would be present.

He was a very tall man, more than six feet, and the breadth of his shoulders and the depth of his chest, slimming down to a lean waist, were in keeping with his splendid height.

His face was as arresting as his form. His rather wide mouth, grin-quirked at the corners, relieved somewhat the touch of fierceness evinced by the prominent hawk nose above and the powerful jaw and chin beneath. His pushed-back hat revealed crisp, thick hair so black that a blue shadow seemed to lie upon it in certain lights.

The striking countenance was dominated by long, black-lashed eyes of very pale gray. Eyes the color of a glacier lake under a stormy sky. Cold, reckless eyes that nevertheless always seemed to have little devils of laughter dancing in their clear depths. Devils that, did occasion warrant, could leap to the front and be anything but laughing, before whose bleak stare armed and plenty salty individuals had been known to quail.

The horse he bestrode was worthy of his unusual master. Full eighteen hands high, his coat was midnight black, his every line bespeaking speed and endurance, his eyes large and liquid, full of fire and intelligence.

A gallant man atop a gallant horse, and the picture was complete.

Thus rode Ranger Walt Slade, named by the *peónes* of the Rio Grande villages, *El Halcón* — The Hawk!

Slade wore the plain efficient garb of the rangeland — Levis, the bibless overalls favored by the cowboys,

4

soft blue shirt with vivid neckerchief looped at his sinewy throat, well scuffed halfboots of softly tanned leather, and the broad-brimmed J. B. hat, the "rainshed" of the plains. And to the homely garb he lent dignity and distinction. All in all, he looked to be an unusually neat chuckline rider, which was just what he wanted to look.

There was one slightly incongruous note to his peaceful attire. Around his waist were double cartridge belts, from the carefully worked and oiled cut-out holsters of which protruded the plain black butts of heavy guns, and from the butts of those big Colt forty-fives, his slender, muscular hands seemed never far away.

"Well, Shadow, getting close," Slade said to the horse. "That smudge against the sky is the smoke from Echo. Mary Merril and her train of carts loaded with casings and other needed materials must be rolling into town about now. Another half hour and we will be jogging through the cut. That is if nothing happens."

Something would happen.

It was a beautiful day of golden sunshine washing a sky of cleanest blue, with not a cloud and only that telltale smudge to mar the serenity and peace. And Slade thoroughly enjoyed the ride over the rangeland grasses that bent their amethyst heads to the caress of a soft and fragrant wind.

However, while attuned to the beauty of his surroundings, Slade rode alert and watchful, for there was no doubt but that a shrewd and ruthless outlaw bunch was plaguing the Sanderson, Tumble, Echo area.

And the outlaws had little use for *El Halcón*, who had dealt summarily with a number of their fraternity. So Slade let no ridge or hill-crest pass without a careful scrutiny. He grew even more alert as he neared the brush-grown crest of the south basin wall.

It was his habitual caution that saved him. That plus a number of birds wheeling and darting over a tall stand of thicket that fringed the lip of the rise to the crest.

It was just a gleam of sunlight reflecting from shifted metal, but it was enough. He was going sideways and down from the saddle even as smoke puffed from the lip of the slope and a bullet whizzed through the space his body had occupied a split second before.

CHAPTER
TWO

As he went down, Slade slid his high-power, long-range Winchester from the saddle boot.

Prone on the ground, he clamped the butt to his shoulder and sprayed the growth with lead.

As he held his trigger finger in abeyance for an instant, his amazingly keen ears caught the sound of a cry, and a beat of fast hoofs dimming west by north.

"Nicked the devil!" he muttered to Shadow.

For moments he lay motionless, eyes fixed on the crest, rifle ready for instant action.

Reassured by the fact that the birds, which had flown higher, were settling back into the thicket, he rose to his feet, still watchful, although he was pretty sure there had been but one drygulcher holed up on the crest with murder in mind.

"Yes, looks like everything is under control," he told Shadow. "Let's go. Perhaps we can make town without further excitement."

Shadow snorted his disgust with the whole loco business and ambled on, the opening of the breakthrough growing plainer by the minute. Half an hour later found Slade riding through the cut.

"And judging from the racket coming out of the bowl, I'd say the boys are starting their celebration a mite soon," he remarked to his bored horse. "Listen to them beller!"

Shadow's snort seemed to say there was no need to listen, that ear plugs were what was needed most.

Passing out the north mouth of the breakthrough, Slade found himself embroiled in a scene of riotous hilarity. The streets and the bars were crowded, and everybody apparently felt it was his bounden duty to make as much noise as the human throat could achieve.

Railroad and oil field workers who recognized him shouted greetings, which he acknowledged with a wave of his hand. However, he did not pause, but kept riding until he reached the quarters of Westbrook Lerner, near the northern slope of the bowl and not far from the north breakthrough. Lerner spotted him approaching and hurried out to greet him.

Lerner was a vigorous little man with a leathery, poreless skin and quick bright eyes. He was wealthy, owning several producing wells in the great Splindletop field near Beaumont. But he was a wildcatter at heart, his greatest thrill the opening of a new field.

Acting on the advice and with the assistance of Walt Slade, he had opened up the Tumble field, and then the Echo. With characteristic generosity he had thrown both fields wide open to everybody, first come first served. Oil men from all over were quick to take advantage of the offer, witness the forest of derricks rising in the great basin, with more being erected.

"My, but I'm glad you managed to make it," he said as he and Slade shook hands with warmth. "And so will Mr. Dunn be when he rolls in tomorrow, as I fully expect him to," Lerner said. "Okay, Shadow first," he added, bestowing a pat on the great black's sleek neck. "To a stall and a helpin' of oats for him."

He let out a shout and his stable keeper, an elderly Mexican, appeared. He had formerly been introduced to Shadow, a one-man horse who allowed no one to lay a hand on him without his master's sanction. Slade knew the horse would be in good hands and would lack for nothing. He shook hands with the keeper and voiced a Spanish greeting, which caused him to smile and bow.

"And now you come in for coffee and something to eat," the oil magnate said to Slade. "Imagine you can use both?"

Slade did not argue the point.

Lerner's quarters were unpretentious but comfortable. A living room with two couch-beds, a dining room and a kitchen. On the second floor were two bedrooms with running water, hot and cold, and a small bath.

The cook, also Mexican, was called in to shake hands and smile and bow and promise an outstanding repast for *El Halcón*.

"And now, Walt, if you don't mind, I'll leave you for a while," Lerner said. "I want to hustle down to the cart station and give Mary Merril a hand with the unloading of the carts. She brought in just about the biggest train ever, today, stuff badly needed. The well owners are all with her, and a lot of their workers, to assist the carters.

They've rigged up flares and will keep on working after it gets dark, until the chore is finished. Don't want anything hanging over tomorrow. I'll stop at the Diehard Saloon and tell Sheriff Crane you're here, if he doesn't already know it. He came in with the cart train."

The cook was as good as his word and Slade enjoyed an excellent dinner, topping it off with a couple of cups of coffee and the same number of cigarettes. After which he headed for the Diehard Saloon, expecting to find Sheriff Tom Crane there, his usual hangout when in Echo. The carts and their owner could come a little later. Right now she was undoubtedly a very busy woman.

As he expected, Slade found the sheriff at the Diehard. They shook hands and sat down at a table that, despite the crowd that packed the place, the owner, Vince Rader, had reserved for him.

"Well, are you slipping?" Crane asked. "Where are the carcasses?"

"If you will look close on the crest, close to the lip of the south slope, you will find some blood spots, I believe," Slade replied. "That's the best I can do for you at present."

"What! What!" exclaimed the sheriff. "What the blankety-blank are you talking about?"

Slade recounted, briefly, the attempted drygulching. The sheriff said things best forgotten.

"And after you right away, eh?" he growled in conclusion.

"Looks a little that way," Slade conceded. "Didn't work, and that's all that really counts. How you been, Tom?"

"I'm fine now," Crane replied. "But, like Mary, I expect to be afflicted with a steady case of the jitters with you around. Never a dull moment with *El Halcón* on the job."

"And let me be away from the section a couple of weeks and you import a new outlaw bunch, according to what the deputies told me," Slade countered. "Just what has been going on, Tom?"

"Oh, the same old story," Crane answered. "Robberies, burglings, shootings. Rumhole in Langtry, held up and robbed. Bartender shot through the arm. Two stores in Sanderson robbed. Owner of one got a split head. Stage coach robbed. Nobody killed, I'm glad to say. Rumhole in Tumble robbed, slick job. Owner grabbed in back room tallying the day's take. Several days, in fact, I learned later. A hefty passel of *dinero* tied onto. Want to hear more?"

"Guess that will hold me for the time being," Slade said. "Any suspects?"

"Nary a one," snorted Crane. "I ain't worried about that anymore, now. You'll mighty quick run a brand on some galoot."

"Thanks for the confidence," Slade smiled. "Hope you're right."

"Never was I wrong where that angle is concerned," the sheriff declared.

"How about descriptions?" Slade asked. "Surely must have gotten some, with all those chores pulled."

11

"You know how that is," answered Crane. "Same old story there — descriptions so vague they're worth practically nothing. Each description I got said there were five of the devils, all wearing whiskers."

"False beards, the chances are," Slade said. "The simplest of disguises, but effective. Everybody on the lookout for whiskers, with the real culprits clean shaven. What else?"

"Seems one of the hellions, the one giving the orders, was big and tall, close to six feet and plenty broad, I gather."

"A description that applies to any number of individuals in this section," was Slade's comment.

"Oh, I suppose so," the sheriff said wearily. "So there's how the situation stands, a sorta' familiar one, wouldn't you say? So let us drink!"

They proceeded to do so, the sheriff a snort of redeye, Slade a cup of fragrant coffee, steaming hot.

"And now," said the sheriff sucking the last drops from his mustache, "don't you figure we'd better amble over to the cart station and see how Mary is making out with her unloading? They've got flares going to provide light and should be finished up not so very long from now. Shall we go?"

"Could do worse, I reckon," *El Halcón* conceded. "Let's be moseying."

Outside they found the streets even more crowded, and quite a bit noisier.

"And this ain't nothing to what's coming," snorted Crane. "Listen to the loco coots beller!"

12

Slade smiled slightly as they wormed their way through the jostling, whooping throng. For he knew that despite his big talk that tended to deplore the hilarity, the rugged oldtimer liked the exuberant excitement of such a night as he, Slade, did, but refused to admit it. Perhaps because he had to uphold the dignity of his office.

However, after considerable shoving and shouldering they reached the cart station in one piece, which was more than the Ranger expected once or twice. They found the unloading going forward apace.

Lerner was there, and standing beside him was a girl. She had a mop of curly, unruly black hair, a lot of it, that caught glints of gold from the flares. Her astonishingly big eyes were the deeply blue of the Texas sky on a summer afternoon. Her sweetly turned lips were the vivid scarlet of the red, red rowan, her complexion creamily tanned by the sun and wind, with a few freckles powdering the bridge of her straight little nose. And even overalls and soft blue flannel shirt could not conceal the luscious curves of her small figure.

All in all, Miss Mary Merril, owner of the cart train was something to quicken the beat of masculine pulses.

In her hands she was riffling a sheaf of check sheets. The sheriff let out a whoop, she glanced toward him. The sheets fluttered in every direction, Westbrook Lerner making frantic grabs for them, as she raced to where Slade stood and hurled herself into his arms.

"Darling! Darling!" she chattered. "I heard you were here and was wondering how long I'd have to wait to see you. Will be finished with the unloading soon and

13

you may escort me to Uncle Westbrook's and give me a chance to clean up a bit, change clothes and rest a little."

"You go right ahead, Mary, and get some rest," said Lerner, who had joined them. "I'll take care of the final odds and ends; really very little more to do. Saxon, the head carter, is collecting the money for the shipments and will stash it in the Diehard safe, where it'll be safe until you are ready to roll to Sanderson day after tomorrow. You go right ahead."

"Thanks, Uncle Westbrook, I will," the girl replied. "I admit I am tired. Has been a long and hard day. Will see you at the Diehard later, Uncle Tom," she told the sheriff. "Come on, Walt."

With her practically tucked under his arm, Slade battled their way to Lerner's quarters. Mary scampered upstairs to her room on the second floor. Slade made himself comfortable with a cup of coffee the old cook brought him, with a low bow to *El Halcón*.

"Take your time, Mary," Slade called to her. "I may go out for a while, but I'll be right with you when you are ready. The cook is fixing your dinner. You'll be able to eat in peace here, which you probably wouldn't at the Diehard. We'll look that rumhole, as the sheriff calls it, over later."

"Okay," came the answer, somewhat muffled because of running water.

Meanwhile, Slade relaxed, or tried to. Outside, the celebration hullabaloo was going strong, and stronger, but in Lerner's quarters all was peace and quiet. Slade saw no reason why he should not relax in comfort.

14

But blast it, he couldn't! Stealing into his thought processes on little cat feet was a presentiment that warned things were not what they seemed to be, that there was trouble of some kind just waiting to develop. He had experienced that sort of a presentiment before and knew better than to just dismiss it as a figment of the imagination, unworthy of any serious consideration.

A hunch? He usually called it that. Sheriff Crane always did. The most aggravating angle was the fact that it was so utterly vague, almost impossible to pin down until the untoward action it warned of was ready to leap into being.

Oh, to heck with it! What is due to happen will happen. Just up to him to handle the situation when it did stick its ugly head around the corner. He'd always made out in the past and very likely would again. Feeling better by the decision, he rolled another cigarette and smoked in untroubled enjoyment. Let the future and its worries take care of themselves!

Lerner arrived, looking complacent. "Everything taken care of," he announced. "The well owners are greatly pleased with the shipments and are clamoring for more. No work tomorrow, however, and the carts won't roll for Sanderson until the next day. Mary wouldn't have her boys miss the breakthrough celebration. She always thinks of them first. That's why they'll go to any lengths to please her, and enjoy doing it."

"Precisely," Slade agreed. "And they are loyal to the core. 'As ye sow, so shall ye reap!' You can't beat the

Scriptures when it comes to always having a passage that fits the occasion exactly."

Mary came bouncing down the stairs. She had changed to a spangled, short dancing skirt and a low-cut bodice. Lerner whistled. Slade twinkled his eyes at her. Under his regard, she drooped her black lashes and her color rose.

"Will I pass at the Diehard?" she asked gaily. "But really, I donned this outfit for Walt, so he won't have any excuse not to dance with me."

"What you want to do," pointedly remarked the sheriff who had just dropped in, "is build up your strength." Mary wrinkled her pert nose at him and refrained from further comment.

Mary got her dinner and declared it was all the cook had promised it would be. Lerner and the sheriff intimated they, too, could go for a small surrounding.

Slade had already eaten and decided to stroll around a little while the others were doing justice to the cook's offerings. He walked slowly to the south mouth of the breakthrough.

Everything was peaceful there, the last of the workers streaming out. For to all practical purposes, the breakthrough was completed with only the laying of the few lengths of steel left to mark the beginning of the celebration with the driving of the last spike.

The workers shouted greetings, which he returned. A foreman paused to talk with him.

"Mr. Broderick, the engineer, told us to go have some fun," the foreman said.

16

"A good notion," Slade agreed. "You have been doing a splendid chore of work, as Mr. Dunn will say when he looks things over tomorrow. And in the special pay envelopes that will be passed out tomorrow you'll find something substantial to denote his pleasure." The workers raised a cheer.

"Of course we all know, Mr. Slade, that you're the real big boss, answerable only to Mr. Dunn. And I want to take this opportunity to say that all the boys are proud to work for such a boss."

"Thank you," Slade replied. "Thank you very much, I greatly appreciate that."

"You've got it coming, Mr. Slade," said the foreman. "Be seeing you, Mr. Slade."

Slade returned to Lerner's quarters and the others were uplifted by the contact. But the blasted hunch that somewhere there was trouble in the making persisted.

CHAPTER
THREE

"Began to fear you had gotten mixed up in something," Mary said.

"Not so far," Slade returned cheerfully. "Everything plumb peaceful."

"Sure don't sound peaceful," growled the sheriff emptying his glass. "Listen to 'em beller!"

"The second time you've said that, Uncle Tom," Mary pointed out. "You love it, and you know you do. But I think we'd better move down to the Diehard, where I can keep a better watch over Walt. Here, the door being so close, it's easy for him to slip out. You coming along, Uncle Westbrook."

"Guess I might as well," conceded Lerner.

Mary slipped on a cloak over her dancing costume and they set out.

After a deal of shoving and nudging and squirming, they made it to the Diehard where Rader had their table reserved for them, per usual.

"Yes, this is better," said Mary, gazing with appreciation at the crowded bar and equally crowded tables.

"Walt, there's a feller at the bar I want to speak to you about," said Crane. "Name's Rice, Van Rice. You'll remember Mort Japley who owned the Bar M spread north of the Echo bowl, of course. You and him got quite friendly. Well, Japley hankered to move east and take up a spread in the Trinity River section, where he has relations. He sold out to Rice not long after you left here last time. That's Rice, about the middle of the bar, the big feller with the sorta bristly hair. Has the look of a salty gent, wouldn't you say?"

"He could be," Slade conceded, "but not necessarily so; you can't judge from appearances."

He regarded the new Bar M owner with interest. He felt he had heard some rather disturbing news. Jaggers Dunn's railroad line to the northwest had to pass over the Bar M holding, and were the owner inimical to the railroad, trouble could result.

Rice was a big man, nearly six feet tall, Slade judged, and thick-set. He had a big nose, a square jaw and a prominent chin. As the sheriff said, his dark hair was inclined to be bristly. Slade was not sure, at that distance, but he believed his eyes were also dark, although they could be dark blue.

"Where is Rice from, do you know?" he asked.

"Like lots of newcomers hereabouts who moved south looking for a better climate, from the Panhandle country," Crane replied. "At least that's what I've been told. Gather he owned a spread up there and sold out."

"I see," Slade said thoughtfully. He himself was well acquainted with the Panhandle section.

"Please," said Mary, "let's forget about Mr. Rice for a while. I want to dance."

Slade smilingly obliged and they slipped onto the floor. Dancing on so crowded a floor was more of an acrobatic venture, but both were outstanding dancers and they made out, even though Mary was rosy and breathing a mite hard after several fast numbers, and glad to plump into a chair by the table for a while.

Outside, abruptly sounded more than the usual racket. The swinging doors banged open and in boomed the carters, their horses and vehicles cared for. Diehard business picked up, decidedly, which a moment before would have been considered impossible, the carters having their own quaint ways of enlivening a place, even one that already was bursting at the seams.

Slade noted that big Van Rice, who had been shoved around a bit, appeared to be smiling indulgently at their antics. A little later, he sauntered out, waving to the sheriff as he passed. Crane returned the greeting.

"Hellion always seems to try to be pleasant," he grumbled grudgingly. Slade smiled, and did not comment.

The hours slipped past, not quietly. The din was deafening, the air thick with smoke. And Slade's trouble hunch kept growing more demanding, although still not assuming anything definite.

But it was making him more restless by the minute. He glanced at the swinging doors. Outside, despite the hullabaloo of the streets, the air would be less smoky. Which would help.

Mary and Lerner were dancing. The sheriff was talking with Vince Rader at the far end of the bar. With

20

another glance around, Slade stood up, hesitated a moment, then slipped through the swinging doors and into the bedlam of the street, where he was immediately engulfed in the bellowing, jostling throng. He chuckled as his big shoulders cleared a way for him.

And it was cooler outside, the air fresh and bracing. A gentle breeze blew from the west, sweeping away the smoke and fumes of the field with its multitude of derricks bristling to the starry sky.

He thought of the breakthrough. Would be even cooler and fresher there, and deserted, peaceful and lonely, a relief from the continuous babble of voices. He turned his steps in that direction.

It was quiet and peaceful in the mouth of the cut. Slade entered and sauntered along beside the rails.

Suddenly he raised his head in an attitude of listening. From ahead, near the north mouth of the cut, had come a sound, a watery mutter, loudening.

He instantly recognized it for what it was, the blower of a locomotive going full blast, where certainly no blower should be operating. He quickened his pace, hands dropping toward the butts of his Colts.

At a dead run he rounded a shallow curve in the cut and saw, at the end of the steel, with the mouth of the breakthrough but a few lengths ahead, a big locomotive, black smoke pouring from its stack, the blower howling. Slade heard the clang of a fire hook on the metal apron of the cab and the rasp of a shovel pouring coal into the roaring furnace.

Even as he rounded the curve, a man with a wrench in his hand, with which he had screwed the safety valve down tight, dropped from the side platform. Two more men dropped from the cab, one slamming the fire door shut. Leaning against the cylinder at the front of the engine was still another man, tall, broad. All four were bearded. Slade's great voice rolled in thunder through the bellow of the blower —

"Up! You are under arrest! In the name of the State of Texas!"

Going sideways in a streaking dive as he heard astounded yelps, saw hands flickering to holsters, he whipped out both Colts and let drive.

One of the wreckers fell. The big man leaning against the cylinder whirled around to the front of the engine and out of sight. Answering shots yelled past the ducking, dodging, slithering Ranger, fanning his face with their lethal breath, twitching the sleeve of his shirt. Both Colts boomed and a second outlaw went down. The remaining devil took deliberate aim. But even as he squeezed trigger, Slade hurled himself down and the slug whined over him. Crouched on the ground he shot, again. And there were three motionless forms lying beside the locomotive, the boiler of which was jumping and quivering as the steam pressure rose.

Slade did not attempt to pursue the big man. To do so would have been crass folly. Besides, there were other matters urgently demanding his attention. He dashed up the gangway steps and into the cab.

A glance at the steam pressure gage told him there was not a moment to lose. The boiler had taken all it could. Should it explode, as to all appearances it would in another moment, both he and everything nearby would be blown into the next county. He seized the grate-shaker bar and began frantically to dump the fire, swinging the fire door wide open in the same ripple of movement.

Acrid fumes rose from the grass scorched by the hot coals dumped on it, but the deadly steam pressure began dropping at once. Slade glanced at the water glass, saw it was fairly high. When it was safe to do so, he turned on the inspirators and raised the water level to where it should be with the banked fire.

Retrieving the engineer's torch from his seatbox, he lighted it and looked things over. Securing the wrench from where it lay beside the dead outlaws, he restored the safety valve to its proper position.

After which he sat down, rolled a cigarette and reviewed the incident, which was slightly similar to one he had experienced during the construction of the Tumble short line.

What was the explanation? To all appearances it had been a seemingly senseless attempt to delay the breakthrough celebration. Would have done that, all right. Had the loco boiler let go, it would have brought down enough of the side slopes to block the cut mouth and require several days of work to clean up the mess. But what would be gained, and by whom? There must be some more serious ulterior motive to be considered. What? Slade didn't have the answer to that, and wished he had.

Finishing his smoke, he raised the water in the boiler to a high level, banked the fire and headed for the Diehard, where by now there would be anxiety aplenty.

The street crowds were thinning out, for it was quite late, and the real celebration would not start until tomorrow. So Slade made good progress.

When he reached the Diehard, he found Crane's deputies, Blount, and Arbaugh, were present. Also present was a tall, slender young man with a dark, savage face and snapping black eyes. It was Estevan, a Yaqui-Mexican knife man, who had ridden from Sanderson. He was one of Slade's closest friends, and one of the most dependable. They had experienced many stirring adventures together. He always liked to be close to Slade, and was whenever possible. For, he would say, where is *Capitán*, the Mexican term of respect, there is always the "fun." The fun, from his understanding of the term, being the hissing music of his flung knife, which never missed.

When Slade entered, he was met by accusing glances from Mary and the sheriff.

"Well, where are they?" Crane asked.

"They?" Slade repeated, questioningly.

"Yes, 'they'," snorted the sheriff. "The carcasses."

"Well, if you're really interested," Slade replied, "you will find three at the north mouth of the breakthrough, beside a locomotive."

"What! What!" barked Crane.

Slade told them briefly of the attempt to blow up the locomotive boiler, to the accompaniment of various exclamations from his hearers.

"Guess you'd better take along some of the carters to help pack the bodies to Lerner's stable and lay them out on the floor there," he concluded.

24

"I'll go right along to supervise the chore," the oil magnate said.

"All right," Slade nodded. "I'll accompany Mary to her room — it's late — and then join you in the cut. "Let's go!"

With the deputies and half a dozen of the carters, who welcomed the chore, Crane and Lerner set out. Estevan glided into the kitchen. Slade knew that he and some of his *amigos* would slip out the back door to make sure for *Capitán* and his *Señorita* the way was clear.

When Slade reached the mouth of the cut, the bodies of the slain outlaws were hauled into the light of a flare and examined. Slade removed the false beards he knew very well they wore, to reveal hard-lined countenances with nothing outstanding about them so far as he could ascertain. All three had been cowhands, but had not done range work for a long time.

"I'll send 'em to Sanderson in a cart, day after tomorrow," Lerner promised.

"That'll be fine," said the sheriff. "Make nice floor decorations. Well, guess that takes care of everything here. Pack 'em to the stable, boys."

"Well, what do you think?" he added to Slade as they headed for Lerner's quarters.

"Frankly, I don't know what to think," Slade admitted. "The whole affair seems utterly senseless. Only one thing I feel sure about."

"What's that?" Crane asked as the Ranger paused.

"That in some way it ties up with trouble somebody has in mind for the railroad. As to what and why, I haven't the slightest notion."

"You'll find out, and soon," the sheriff predicted cheerfully. "Well, I'm going to turn off here," he said as they reached the south mouth of the cut. "I'll be sleeping at Rader's place tonight, per usual. Good night, Walt."

"Good night, Tom," *El Halcón* said as he headed for Lerner's quarters.

Pretty well tired out by a long and exciting day, he too called it a night.

CHAPTER
FOUR

The day dawned beautifully, with promise of the weather cooperating to make the breakthrough celebration a success. Mary and Lerner still had some work to do on the check sheets, so Slade headed for the Diehard to commune with the sheriff, whom he found placidly puffing his pipe with a snort before him.

Although it was still early, the Diehard was already doing business, as were the other saloons. More and more people were appearing on the streets. Soon the railroaders and the carters would receive their bonus envelopes and the celebration would really begin to get under way.

"Found quite a bit of money in the pockets of those three horned toads," Crane remarked apropos the three dead outlaws. "Rader has it stashed in his safe. Oh, the devils have been doing all right by themselves. Guess they won't enjoy such prosperity with *El Halcón* on the job. Anybody taken another shot at you?"

"Not so far," Slade replied composedly. "The one try from the crest the only one."

"Reckon they'll learn soon that trying to drygulch *El Halcón* is a losing proposition.

"Just the same, although I admit it has something to be said in its favor, that *El Halcón* business worries me, you sashaying around and continually getting into ruckuses without Ranger prestige to back you up," he added querulously.

Owing to his habit of working alone whenever possible, and often not revealing his Ranger connections, Walt Slade had acquired a peculiarly conflicting dual reputation. Those who knew the truth declaring he was not only the most fearless of the Rangers but the ablest as well. While others, knowing him only as *El Halcón* with killings to his credit, insisted as vehemently that he was himself just an owlhoot too smart to get caught, so far.

Among this latter group he had vigorous supporters as well as detractors, who pointed out that he always worked on the side of law and order and that sheriffs and other peace officers of impeccable repute gladly welcomed his assistance when the going got rough.

The deception worried Captain McNelty who feared his ace undercover man might come to harm at the hands of some mistaken sheriff or other law enforcement officer Slade would be loath to kill and would endanger his own life trying not to.

To say nothing of a professional gunslinger who hoped to enhance his own dubious fame by downing the fastest gunhand in the whole Southwest, and not above shooting in the back to achieve his aims. Although Captain Jim would be first to concede that the gentleman would almost certainly just acquire six feet of earth eight feet down as a reward for his efforts.

"Slipping up behind Walt is like slipping up behind a rabbit," the Ranger Commander was wont to say. Those eyes of his can see in all directions at once.

When Slade would point out that as *El Halcón* there were open to him certain avenues of information that would be closed to a known Ranger, and that outlaws thinking him one of their own brand would get careless sometimes, to their grief Captain Jim would fuss and grumble but not forbid the deception and Slade would go his careless way as *El Halcón*, satisfied with the present and bothering about the future not at all, and treasuring most what was said by the *peónes* and other humble folk —

"*El Halcón! El Halcón*, the good, the just, the compassionate, the friend of the lowly and all who know sorrow or oppression! May *El Diós* ever guard him!"

Walt Slade firmly believed that such a prayer, winging its way to the foot of the Throne, would stand like a shield between a man and harm.

"By the way," remarked the sheriff, "there's another newcomer who 'pears to be doing all right by himself. Showed up here not long after Van Rice, the new owner of the Bar M I pointed out to you last night. He's a builder. Set up a few stores, the owner's well pleased with them. He hires mostly Mexican help, who are tops at that sort of work."

"What's his name?" Slade asked.

"Messa, Lance Messa," the sheriff replied. "Speaks well and gets along with people."

Slade regarded the builder with interest. All newcomers to a section interested *El Halcón*, especially if it appeared they were taking up permanent residence.

Messa was as tall as Rice, but not so powerfully built. He had straight features, dark brown hair and rather pale blue eyes. His movements were graceful and assured. Without a doubt an able man who very likely accomplished whatever he set his hand to.

Mary and Lerner arrived. The girl's cheeks were rosy, her eyes sparkling, her expression gay and animated.

"Hmmm!" said the sheriff. "You look as if you had a really good — rest!"

"Never mind the sly remarks," she retorted. "Uncle Westbrook's cook gave me an excellent breakfast, but that was quite a while ago. I crave a snack. I'm hungry!"

Rader hurried to the kitchen. The sheriff chuckled, twinkled his eyes at her, and ordered another snort.

The Diehard was filling up. The musicians filed in and occupied their platform. The dance floor girls scampered in from their dressing room. The faro bank and the roulette wheels got set for business.

The carters arrived like a miniature, not too miniature, hurricane. Saxon began distributing the bonus envelopes Mary had given him. Louder whoops were raised, and cheers, and tumultuous greetings for Mary and Slade, and everybody else.

Saxon, the head carter, asked Mary to dance. The sheriff moved to the far end of the bar for a few words with Rader. Slade and Lerner were left alone for the time being.

"Walt," the magnate said, "I've been thinking more and more about what you had to say about that big pool to the north. I believe that with the new rotary drills they're perfecting it would be possible to tap that pool. It would require a very large outlay of capital, but would pay off tremendously. What do you think?"

"I think it could be done," *El Halcón* replied. "The operation would be costly, but it would indeed pay off tremendously. However, let it ride for the present. Give me a chance to do a little investigating. Most of that pool lies under the Bar M holding, and Rice, the new Bar M owner, is still an uncertain quantity. We don't know just what would be his reaction, and it would be of great advantage to obtain his cooperation."

"Think there might be difficulty in swinging him into line?" Lerner asked.

"Frankly, I don't know at the moment," Slade said. "He is an oldtime cattleman and many of them are violently opposed to such operations, including even the railroad. Incidently, there is another angle to consider. We may not be the only ones who have such a project in mind, or quickly would have did they learn the truth. Say an outfit like the M.K. Railroad System, Jaggers Dunn's rival, who understands ethics as just a word in the dictionary and don't trouble their heads about them."

"I see," nodded Lerner. "So we don't want any loose talking for the wrong pair of ears to tie onto."

"Exactly," Slade agreed. "We can trust for sure Mary, the sheriff and his deputies, and Estevan. Trust them to be circumspect, too, but that's as far as we should really go. With a couple of exceptions, of course, Mr. Dunn, and Charley, the president of the Sanderson bank. We can count on their backing to the hilt."

"Right!" said Lerner. "Now we are all lined up. As the sheriff would say —"

"Let us drink!"

CHAPTER
FIVE

After a bit, Lerner joined some well owners who wished to discuss certain matters with him. Mary was on the floor, the sheriff still talking with Rader. And Slade was growing restless. He took to the streets again, wondering if another trouble hunch was developing. Not so far, it seemed, but he was not positive. The darn things were uncanny in the way they developed from nothing. They weren't, then all of a sudden they were.

Which did not tend to enhance one's peace of mind. Like waiting for the gent in the room upstairs to drop the other shoe. A hackneyed old expression but not altogether without meaning.

Suddenly he had an inspiration. He turned and wormed his way through the crowd back to the Diehard.

I'm going up to the head of the breakthrough," he told Mary and the sheriff. "Mr. Dunn will be here any time now. They'll roll his car right to the end of the steel and I want to be there when he arrives. And I'm going to ride Shadow and give him a chance to see the fun."

"Sure he won't be bored?" cautioned the sheriff.

"I don't think so," Slade replied. "He'll understand what's going on as well as you and I."

"That I don't doubt one bit," said Crane.

"We'll be up there with Mr. Lerner, very soon," Mary said. "Be careful, dear, and don't get stepped on. My feet are still sore from last night."

"I'll let Shadow do the stepping on," Slade answered cheerfully. "He's an expert at that."

Without mishap, he reached the stable and cinched up. Leading the big black out, he swung into the saddle. Shadow, who hated to be confined and inactive, snorted gaily and slugged his head above the bit.

Riding at a fair pace, Slade reached the north mouth of the breakthrough, where the railroaders were already gathering. They shouted greetings, as did Broderick, the construction engineer. Slade returned the greetings and rode on through the cut to the open prairie.

Reining in, he studied the terrain in every direction. For the hunch was beginning to function. Yes, somewhere nearby there was trouble in the making.

Some five hundred yards to the north, perhaps a little more, was a low hill with steep side slopes, its crest heavily brush-grown. Slade studied it with interest. He instinctively went sideways in the saddle as he saw smoke puff at the upper edge of the slope.

But the slug whined past well overhead. Another puff, another lethal whine, lower. A third, just a trifle too low for comfort. Looked like the hellion holed up in the growth might mean business. Slade whipped his high-power Winchester from the saddle boot and let drive just above where he noted the smoke puffs. Again

34

and again he squeezed trigger, each time dropping the rifle muzzle a trifle, until his bullets were slashing through the growth just a little ways above where the smoke puffed. Did the hidden drygulcher really mean business, the gun battle was under way.

The top of the brush was greatly agitated, as though a speeding horse were brushing the slender trunks. Slade could follow the drygulcher's progress by the swaying tops; he was certainly going away from there, and fast. Did he hold to his present course he would pass close to the Bar M ranch house. But there were plenty of places where he could turn off in some other direction.

For a moment, Slade contemplated trying to run him down, but decided against it, feeling that he would be of better use right where he was.

The railroaders were wildly excited, shouting, cursing. Broderick came running to Slade, yammering questions.

"Looks like a senseless attempt to mar or delay the breakthrough celebration," Slade told him. "But I don't think you need worry about any more drygulching from that hill today. Looked like the devil didn't intend to kill, but as to that I'm not sure. Was very long shooting for an ordinary rifle and perhaps he just misjudged his elevation a trifle. Anyhow he's gone, with no harm done so far as I can see. Should be peaceful enough when Mr. Dunn gets here which should be soon now."

"I'd say the devil didn't figure on you being here with that Winchester of yours," growled Broderick. "Here comes the sheriff, and Lerner and Miss Merril.

Guess they speeded up a bit when they heard the shooting."

Which was so. Crane demanded to know what was going on. Broderick told him, in detail. The sheriff swore, under his mustache, in respect to Mary's presence. She shook her shining curls.

"Out of my sight a minute and into trouble," she said. "Here comes Estevan, mighty put out at missing the 'fun', as he calls it. Didn't I hear a whistle down toward the south? That should be Mr. Dunn."

Up from the south boomed a big locomotive drawing a single coach, a long green and gold splendor with Winona stenciled on the sides, General Manager Dunn's palatial private car.

As was said of Walt Slade, where Shadow is, there is Slade, it could be said of Jaggers Dunn, where the Winona is, there is Dunn. He spent more time in it than he did at home.

The short train was rolled along one of the sidings to the end of the steel. Dunn was on the front platform, waving, shouting, the sun glinting on the glorious crinkly white mane sweeping back from his big dome-shaped forehead. First thing he beckoned Slade, who moved Shadow in close to the platform to grip the big hairy paw extended to him and then shake hands with Old Sam, the G.M.'s colored porter, chef and general factotum, an old *amigo*.

"Well, see you are right on the job, per usual," Dunn said. "How are you, Walt?"

"Nothing to complain about," Slade replied. "And you?"

36

"Just fine," answered the G.M. "You can brief me on everything later." He shook hands with Lerner, the sheriff, and others, twinkled his eyes at Mary who blushed under his amused regard.

Now the cut was crowded with railroaders, carters, and citizens of Echo. Cross ties thumped, rails clanged, spike mauls thudded. The steel crept slowly forward, the loco and the private car keeping pace. Just a few more rail lengths and the steel would be out on the prairie, where the machine shops, roundhouse, and big assembly yard were already under construction. Construction that would be greatly sped up when it would no longer be necessary to drag the materials up the slope, across the crest and down the far sag.

Rail after rail was swung into place, securely spiked to the ties. The steel was now out on the open rangeland. Broderick held up a gleaming silver spike, the long time symbol of a completed project. Jaggers Dunn dropped from his car, accepted the spike and the maul, tools with which he had been plenty acquainted in his younger days. He placed the spike, swung the maul to crash down on the spike head. With the spike almost all the way in the tie, he handed the maul to Slade who tapped the spike a couple of times, passed the maul to Broderick who did likewise.

The general manager accepted the maul. His big shoulders heaved as down came the maul in the final stroke that drove the spike home.

A cheer went up that shook the hills. Dunn cast the maul aside, straightened his back and flashed teeth almost as white and even as Slade's own in a pleased grin. The old Empire Builder had consummated another project. Now the run to the Fort Stockton area and the drive to Alpine and a hookup with the East-West line, in the operation of which Dunn also had a hand. He returned to his car, beckoning Slade to join him.

"Be seeing you at the Diehard later," Slade told Mary and Lerner and the sheriff. Broderick would stick around until the G.M.'s car pulled out.

"Sam, break out coffee and a bottle," Dunn told old Sam who hastened to fill the "Boss Man's" order. Dunn regarded Slade expectantly.

Beginning with his arrival at the bowl, Slade recounted his experiences. Dunn listened with interest.

"And what do you figure is back of it all?" he asked when the Ranger paused.

"Frankly I don't know for sure just what is back of it," Slade admitted. "It could be an attempt to make trouble for the railroad. Then again it might be just a personal matter, in a way, a couple of tries at eliminating me, which didn't work."

"Would have worked with anybody else," the magnate grunted when the Ranger paused. "And you don't know for sure just where the new Bar M owner stands?"

"Again, no," Slade said. "Of course I intend to try and find out."

"You'll find out, all right," Dunn nodded, sampling the drink Sam placed before him. "And then we'll govern our actions accordingly. As you know, I prefer not to invoke Eminent Domain if I can possibly refrain from doing so. I like to get along with the folks across whose land the road passes, and Eminent Domain seldom makes for good feeling. I'm counting on you to handle that angle. Of course you know that Captain McNelty has agreed to you lending me a hand so long as doing so doesn't interfere with your other chores."

"Yes, I know that," Slade conceded. "Well, it's always worked out in the past, and I don't see any reason why it won't in this instance. The other chores? Oh, just a routine heck raising by an outlaw bunch that has squatted in the section. With the help of Sheriff Crane and his boys, and Estevan, I figure they will be taken care of."

"You're right, they will," chuckled Dunn. "Well, here comes your coffee. Get on the outside of it. A little later and I'll have to be rolling. Meeting in Chicago day after tomorrow I must attend, but I'll be back in a few days, I hope."

"I took the liberty of ordering Broderick to have a couple of his railroad police ride with your car until you hook up with the East-West line south of Tumble."

"Thanks," Dunn said. "Doubt there'll be any use for them, but it was nice of you to think of it. Tell everybody so long for me. And Rader, the Diehard owner, hello. I like him. And Walt, when are you going to stop mavericking around and join up with me, to take over this railroad empire?"

"Before long, I expect," Slade replied. But even as he spoke, Dunn saw born in his steady eyes a look he knew all too well, the look that visioned the lonely trail, the next hilltop, and what might lie beyond. He sighed, but he understood. For many years before, when he had not yet dreamed of a railroad empire, Jaggers Dunn had himself been a rider of the purple sage. He shrugged his big shoulders, emptied his glass.

"Sorry I can't stay for more of the celebration, but to coin a new phrase, business is business," he chuckled. Slade drained his cup. They shook hands with vigor. Slade called goodnight to Sam, the porter, and left the car. He walked to where Shadow stood, looking meditative, possibly visioning oats in the offing, swung into the saddle and headed for Lerner's stable, where he made sure the big black lacked for nothing. Then he started on his walk to the Diehard, shoving his way through the crowds that packed the streets. For now the celebration was really beginning to go strong.

He received a rousing welcome from the carters and others as he entered the saloon.

"Wonderful!" Mary exclaimed. "You actually got here without getting mixed up in something, or did you? Let's hear about it."

"I'm being maligned," he protested. "You know very well I never go looking for trouble." Miss Merril did not appear impressed.

As the private car rolled past the Diehard to pass through Tumble and be coupled to the East-West Flyer, Jaggers Dunn sighed and shook his head.

"The best engineer that ever rode across Texas going to waste," he observed to Sam.

"Boss Man, you're plumb right," the porter agreed.

CHAPTER
SIX

Neither was too much off the beam. Shortly before the death of his father, which occurred after financial reverses that entailed the loss of the elder Slade's ranch, young Walt had graduated with high honors from a famed college of engineering. He had hoped to take a postgraduate course in certain subjects to round out his education and better fit him for the profession he planned to make his life's work.

This, however, became impossible for the time being and Slade was sort of at loose ends, not being sure which way to turn. So when Captain Jim McNelty, the famous Commander of the Border Battalion of the Texas Rangers, with whom Slade had worked some during summer vacations, suggested that he sign up with the Rangers for a while and complete his studies in spare time, Slade lent a receptive ear.

So Walt Slade became a Texas Ranger. Long since he had gotten more from private study than he could have hoped for from the postgrad, was eminently fitted for the profession of engineering, and had received offers of lucrative employment from such giants of the railroad, business, and financial worlds as Jaggers Dunn, oil millionaire and former Governor of Texas

Jim Hogg, and John Warne "Bet a Million" Gates of Wall Street.

But meanwhile, Ranger work had gotten a strong hold on him, providing as it did so many opportunities to help the deserving, bring malefactors to justice, right wrongs, and make his land an even better land for good people. He was loath to sever connections with the illustrious body of law enforcement officers. He was young. Plenty of time to become an engineer. He would stick with the Rangers a while longer. Which was probably what shrewd old Captain McNelty figured would happen.

Now the breakthrough celebration was really under way. The streets were even more crowded than the night before, and so were the bars, which was saying plenty. Song, laughter and clouds of whirling words boiled over the swinging doors. Again high heels clicked and boots thumped, with bottle necks clinking on glass rims.

The roulette wheels were spinning, the little balls jumping from slot to slot. "Around she goes and around she goes! Where she'll stop nobody knows! Except the devil, and he won't tell!"

"It's wild and rowdy, but I love it," declared Mary Merril. "This is going to be the night of nights. Don't you think so, Uncle Tom?"

"It's liable to be most anything before the night is over," replied the sheriff. "Well, the deputies and a couple of specials I managed to hire are keeping an eye on things. So I guess we'll make out. How about you, Walt?"

42

"I just wish to relax and take it easy for a while," *El Halcón* answered. "Which reminds me, it's been a long time since breakfast."

"And I'm starved," Mary wailed.

"Waiter!" shouted the sheriff.

They got their dinner, and managed to eat it despite their madhouse surroundings. The sheriff stuffed his pipe, Slade rolled a cigarette, Mary indulged in a glass of wine.

"I feel like a cat that's just lapped a saucer of milk and sees the door to the canary's cage open," she said. "All's well with the world."

"Hope it stays that way," said Crane. "I'm feeling in a relaxing notion, too."

Lerner dropped in. He had already eaten, but joined them in a drink. He and Slade discussed matters a little.

One incident in which he was embroiled had caused Slade and Dunn to do some puzzling — the attempt to explode the locomotive boiler. It seemed such a senseless thing to do. What could anybody gain by delaying the breakthrough celebration a day or two? Slade wondered, could it have been the beginning of a reign of terror directed against the railroad. He didn't know and wished he did. Of course it could have been but an act of pure cussedness on somebody's part. But Slade was not prepared to accept that convenient explanation. He resolved to go deeper into the matter.

"There's Messa, the builder, talking with Rader," the sheriff remarked. "And about midway along the bar is Van Rice, the new Bar M owner. 'Pears when you see

43

one of those jiggers you see the other. Makes three times, I recall, that they're in here together. Don't seem to know each other, though; never talk together."

"The Diehard is popular," Slade pointed out. "Not so strange that they should like it."

"Guess that's so," agreed Crane, in a rather grudging voice. Slade smiled slightly. He had a feeling the oldtimer might be getting notions about the two gentlemen.

Regarding Van Rice, he was again inclined to agree with the sheriff that the Bar M owner could be plenty salty did he think it advisable to be so. Messa, on the other hand, appeared to be more of the quiet sort, although Slade believed he would be able to take care of himself did it become necessary. He dismissed the pair from his mind. He had other things to think about. Mary hauled him out of his abstracted mood.

"I want to dance," she said.

"Okay," he agreed. "Only it will be more of a wrestling match than a dance. Look at that floor!"

"I like to wrestle," the big-eyed girl giggled.

"And that I don't doubt one bit," declared the sheriff. Mary favored him with a disdainful glance. She and Slade moved onto the crowded floor.

There was indeed hardly room to shuffle, and after three "Wrestles" even Mary was willing to admit she'd had enough of the dance floor for the time being.

It looked like Mary's prediction of the night of nights was no misnomer. For now the celebration was in full swing, the air thick with smoke, the din deafening, glasses beating a tattoo on the bar.

44

"If the roof don't cave in I'll be surprised," said the sheriff. "Whoever heard such a racket! Worse than a Sanderson payday bust for fair."

Lance Messa exchanged a few final words with Rader, wormed his way through the crowd and out the swinging doors, waving to the sheriff as he passed. A few minutes later, Van Rice also departed, also waving.

"I'm going over to gab with Rader a little," said Crane. "See if he knows anything of interest. Wonder where Estevan is?"

"Out scouting around, the chances are," Slade replied. "Maybe in the kitchen, although I rather think he's out."

Lerner persuaded Mary to take a chance on the dance floor again. Slade was left alone with his thoughts.

Although it didn't seem possible that it could, the noise seemed to be increasing, the smoke thickening a bit more. Abruptly *El Halcón* decided he'd had enough of it for a while. He slipped through the swinging doors to the almost-as-badly-packed street. However, there was less smoke, more room for the racket to dissipate, which helped.

He hesitated a moment then began shouldering and shoving his way north. After quite a battle, he reached the mouth of the breakthrough, and paused. It was dark, silent and deserted. Well, there was no locomotive in there tonight. He sat down on a crosstie and gave himself over to meditation, the fresh air and the comparative quiet being inspiring.

For quite a while, he sat there. He smoked a leisurely cigarette. Finally he pinched out the butt, straightened up and tackled the streets again, heading south. He had developed a notion to watch the train from Tumble and the East-West line, which was due shortly, to roll in.

After another scramble, he reached the railroad station where he leaned against a convenient wall and waited. He had time to roll and smoke another cigarette before he heard a whistle note welling from the south. A headlight beam split the darkness and the little train rolled in, ground to a halt. Slade watched the doors. Sometimes passengers from that train interested him.

Tonight immediately proved to be one of those nights. Three individuals who at once interested him left the train. One was an elderly well owner he knew by sight. He carried a large gripsack. Flanking him on either side were two alert looking individuals with hands close to gun holsters.

The trio left the station platform and almost immediately turned into a gloomy side street that led away from the field. On it, buildings were being erected.

They walked purposely, not hurrying. Evidently they knew exactly where they were going, and their destination, for they did not hesitate but kept right on going. And on the far side of the street, in the shadow of buildings, *El Halcón* drifted along behind them.

They were quite some little distance from the station and passing a partly constructed building when the trio plunged forward with startled yells and vanished to above their waists, clawing and scrambling.

And from the dark door of the incompleted building bulged four bearded men, one tall and broad, shooting at the well owner and his two guards as they came.

46

Bounding ahead, Slade streaked out both Colts and let drive. One of the robbers fell. The other three whirled in his direction and answered his fire. Ducking, weaving, slithering, he raced into the blaze of the outlaw guns.

It was almost blind shooting, but another devil went down. The others lined sights on their illusive target.

Slade heard a quick step behind him. Looked like he was surrounded. Curtains!

CHAPTER
SEVEN

But through the shadows streaked a lance of light, and a third outlaw went down with a gurgling scream. The one remaining, the big man, darted into the dark doorway from which he had emerged. Slade started to race in pursuit, but from the shallow excavation into which the well owner and the guards had fallen came gasping cries of pain.

"Hold it!" Slade called. "I'll be with you in a minute. This is the Law speaking, Sheriff Crane's deputy."

"And this, *Capitán*, is I," said Estevan behind him. "I *Capitán* saw and followed. My blade it drank."

"And you came in mighty handy," Slade told him. "Began to look like I was a goner. Strike some matches and let's see what damage to the folks in that hole."

A quick examination showed one guard with a creased scalp, the other with a bullet-slashed upper arm that was bleeding profusely. The yammering well owner was unhurt and came climbing out of the pit, gripping his gripsack.

"Estevan, hightail to the Diehard, it's close, and fetch what you know I'll need. Rader has everything in his back room. Tie onto the sheriff and some of the carters. Just a minute. Here, catch," Slade said.

Dropping into the excavation over which a dark tarpaulin had been spread, making it invisible in the gloom, he picked up the guard with the wounded arm and passed him to the wiry Yaqui-Mexican who received him with ease. The other guard, not badly hurt, was swearing and groaning. With the well owner's help, he climbed out of the hole.

Slade laid the badly wounded guard on the ground, quickly fashioned a tourniquet with his neckerchief and a gun barrel and stanched the flow of blood. Estevan had darted away, heading for the Diehard at racing speed.

"Might have known it! Might have known it!" exclaimed the well owner. "Mr. Slade! Might have known it! Always you are where you're needed most."

"Money in that grip?" Slade asked.

"Plenty," replied the owner. "Sale money for several folks. You saved plenty of *dinero* and, I've a prime notion, three lives. I don't think those sidewinders would have left us alive to witness against them. How in the world did they drop us in that hole?

Slade told him, manipulating the tourniquet as he talked. The owner outdid the scalp-creased and very angry guard at swearing.

In a surprisingly short time, Estevan returned with antiseptic, bandage and tape. Slade quickly had the wound smeared with the salve, heavy pads taped and bandaged, the bleeding stopped.

"That should hold you until we get the doctor down from Sanderson to look you over," Slade told the grateful recipient of his ministrations. "I don't think you'll suffer any permanent harm."

"Take him home and put him to bed," he told the owner and the other guard. "I'll give him a look later in the day." The order was obeyed at once.

Slade had just finished his work on the guard when the sheriff arrived, with him Mary Merril, Lerner, and a dozen or more highly excited carters, including Saxon, the head carter. They were pressed into service to pack the three bodies to Lerner's stable, to be placed alongside the ones already there.

"At this rate, there'll soon be no room for the horses," Crane chuckled. "Fine! Plumb fine!"

"Out of my sight a minute," sighed Mary. "Didn't I tell you this was going to be a night of nights?"

"Not such a bad one, though," Slade replied cheerfully. "Could have been a lot worse, especially if it hadn't been for Estevan dropping out of the sky at just the right moment."

"Saving three lives makes it really worth while," was the girl's sober rejoinder. "And I'll kiss Estevan, if somebody will please hold him. I think the only thing in the world he's afraid of is a woman."

Which gave rise to a general laugh in which even Estevan, rather sheepishly, joined.

"Oh, I don't know," said the sheriff. "I've seen him slant a look toward the dance floor every now and then." More laughter.

Crane glanced around. "That shack the devils holed up in is one of the buildings Lance Messa is erecting," he remarked. Slade nodded, his eyes thoughtful.

50

"You kept the sidewinders from getting a mighty hefty haul," Lerner said. "I know that well owner who was packing the *dinero*. He owns several producing wells and handles financial and sales matters for several of his neighbors. Oil is in demand, and if you are right there with tanks and ready to do business cash on the barrel head, you can drive some good bargains. He makes the trip east and back regularly. Which I reckon the outlaws noted."

"A perfect setup for a shrewd bunch," Slade replied. "The time, the place, everything under control."

"Except *El Halcón*," Lerner pointed out. "That's where they made their little slip." Slade smiled and didn't argue.

"They ain't seen nothin' yet," the sheriff said blithely. "Well, don't see as there is anything else we can do here, so let's amble back to the Diehard for a while before we call it a night. Right now I crave a snort."

"And I'm hungry again," said Mary.

"A snack and some coffee wouldn't go bad," Slade agreed.

"I told the boys to sleep as long as they wish to," Mary added as they got under way. "We won't roll the carts to Sanderson until afternoon. Going to ride with us, Walt?"

"I rather think so," Slade answered. "Got a notion Sanderson can stand a looking over about now."

The streets were not so crowded now, for it was late. The same applied to the Diehard, although it was still doing considerable business. The companions put in their orders and took their time over them. The waiter smiled delightedly at the very generous tip Slade slipped into his palm, and bowed low. Slade had a word of praise for him and the kitchen help. Estevan paused long enough to drink a glass of wine, then glided to the kitchen, and doubtless out the back door to keep an eye on things and clear the way for *El Halcón*. The carters boomed out, other patrons following. Everybody called it a night.

Around noon, Slade visited the wounded guard, dressed the injury and was satisfied with his progress. A wire had been sent the doctor in Sanderson and he would arrive shortly to look after the patient. Slade had also given attention to the other guard's slightly-split scalp, which was trifling.

A couple of hours later the long cart train rolled for Sanderson. With it rode Slade, Estevan, and the sheriff, Saxon the head carter, treasuring the money poke in his lap, beside his ready rifle. He had not forgotten the lecture Slade read him on a former occasion, when he was a mite careless, and took no chances on a repeat.

With the trail passing through four lines of thickly wooded breaks, Slade and Estevan were watchful and alert, scouting ahead, scanning the prairie in every direction, studying every hilltop. The outlaws had proven themselves daring and resourceful, and there was plenty of money in Saxon's poke.

Mary rode Rojo, her big red sorrel, almost as fine a horse as Shadow, but not quite. She was gay and animated, confident that they would reach Sanderson without untoward incident.

52

It was a bright and sunny day, but far to the southeast a line of dark clouds lay on the horizon. The Gulf of Mexico was in that direction, and the Gulf was a most unpredictable body of water, capable of kicking up a bad storm with little advance notice. However, Slade believed that if a storm did break it would not do so until after they reached the railroad town. Then let it do its darndest; he had witnessed that before.

Through the first line of breaks rolled the cart train, through somber shadows, then out again onto the sunny rangeland, with no sign of life except clumps of fat cattle grazing in the distance, and birds fluttering in and out of the thickets.

The second of the breaks was a repeat of the first. Slade dropped back a little, signaled the carts to speed up a bit, then rode on.

The third breaks; but now the lower edge of the sun was touching the horizon, the rising cloud bank beginning to obscure the orb. When they passed through the third breaks and onto the rangeland again, the only light was from the glimmer of stars in the already slightly overcast sky.

"Here's where it will happen, if it does happen, and I've a hunch it will," he told Estevan. "Just a little ways past where the trail enters the brush."

"Doubtless *Capitán* is right," the knife man replied composedly, as he moved his sturdy and intelligent mustang a little closer to Shadow.

Slade also felt he was right, and he didn't like the situation at all. In the darkness, conditions favored the outlaws. Let he and Estevan make one slip and the result would be disastrous. He knew approximately where he believed the attempt would be made but was not quite sure as to the exact location, not in the all embracing gloom. He slowed the pace a bit, straining his ears to catch the slightest alien sound.

As has often happened in the past, it was one of Slade's feathered friends, an owl, that gave the warning. He had been whistling blithely a short distance ahead. Suddenly his carefree whistle changed to a querulous whine. Slade instantly drew rein, Estevan jostling to a halt beside him.

"They're here, right ahead," he whispered to the knife man. "Here, at the beginning of the bend, we must leave the horses; they'll both stand and keep quiet. Ease them into the brush. Right! Now ahead on foot."

The maneuver was executed without a hitch. Step by slow step, hardly daring to breathe, Slade and the knife man eased along through the growth, to almost the apex of the curve, halting abruptly at the jingle of a bit iron and the sound of rough voices. A few more cautious steps and they saw the outlaws, four of them, sitting their horses at the edge of the brush, barely discernible in the clustering shadows. And from the east came the grind of steel tires on the hard surface of the trail. Slade touched Estevan on the shoulder and called softly —

"Figure to hitch a ride, gents?"

There was a storm of startled cries, a blaze of guns. Bullets clipped leaves and twigs from the growth above where Slade and Estevan crouched.

54

Slade flickered both Colts from their sheaths and answered the fire. A groan and the thud of something falling echoed the reports. He tightened his fingers on the triggers, lined sights with the barely seen forms. Then was nearly knocked off his feet.

A crackling explosion! A shriek of agony! Then the screams of terrified horses and a pound of frantic hoofs heading westward. Slade emptied one gun in the direction of the sound, ceased firing as the lead cart of the train swerved around the bend, jostling to a halt. Slade's great voice rolled in thunder through the turmoil that ensued.

"Everything under control," he shouted. "Break out lanterns and let's see what's what."

The lighted lanterns were quickly brought. Their light revealed two bodies lying in the trail, one drilled dead center, the other horribly mutilated, nearly all its face blown away.

"For the love of Pete, what happened?" asked the sheriff.

"A third or a half of a stick of dynamite, from the sound," Slade explained. "Capped and fused and lighted, ready to toss in front of the lead cart horses. Guess the devil held onto it a second too long. His right hand is gone completely."

"Fine!" chortled the sheriff. "Plumb fine! More nice floor decorations for Doc to hold an inquest on. Things are getting better all the time."

Mary joined them. She shuddered at sight of the mangled corpse.

"It's horrible, but you had no choice," she said. "They got exactly what was coming to them."

Miss Merril was not one to cringe before the facts.

"Well, load them into a cart and let's be moving along," Slade ordered.

"Right!" said Crane. "I hanker for a snort. And it looks like it might rain hard pretty soon."

"And I suppose it's terrible to say, after what I've been looking at," said Mary, "but I'm hungry!"

"A gal to ride the river with!" boomed the sheriff. A cheer went up at the conferring of the highest compliment the rangeland can pay.

The bodies were loaded, the carts rolled on. Slade and Estevan were still watchful, although they did not really expect further excitement. They retrieved their horses and rode in front of the train.

Soon the lights of Sanderson glittered through the murk. Without mishap, the cart station was reached. Horses and vehicles were cared for, the bodies packed to the sheriff's office and after cleaning up a bit, everybody boiled into Hardrock Hogan's Branding Pen Saloon for badly needed nourishment, liquid or otherwise.

CHAPTER
EIGHT

The Branding Pen was big and brightly lighted, and tastefully furnished from its long, shining bar to its spotlessly clean lunch counter. The dance floor was commodious, the girls young and pretty, and square shooters from the word go; Hardrock would have no other kind. There were tables for leisurely dinners, others for games. There were two roulette wheels and a faro bank.

Hardrock was a former miner and prospector who had made a good strike and invested the proceeds in the Branding Pen and made a real strike, the place being a money maker from the start, and remaining the most popular place of its kind in Sanderson. Hardrock would have been a wealthy man did he not give away so much money to folks who needed it.

In appearance, Hardrock was no Lily-of-the-Valley or Rose of Sharon. He was big and burly, with an underslung jaw, a wide mouth, bristling red hair and narrowed eyes of palest green. But he was a square shooter in every sense of the word and Walt Slade respected him and liked him very much.

He had an uproarious welcome for Slade and his party and escorted them to Slade's favorite table, always reserved for him when he was in Sanderson.

After shaking hands, he hurried to the kitchen to tell the cook to throw together a surrounding commensurate with the occasion.

At the bar, the carters were entertaining the other patrons with a lurid account of the excitement on the trail. Admiring glances were bent on Slade, but Hardrock would allow nobody to bother him while he was eating.

The cook came through in fine fashion and his offering was stowed away with gusto, everybody risking a second helping. Then Slade rolled a cigarette, the sheriff charged his pipe. Estevan paused long enough to accept a glass of wine and glided to the kitchen to eat with his friends there.

"And now, if you'll walk me to the hotel, I'll really clean up and rest a while," Mary said. "You and Uncle Tom will have matters to discuss at the office, and then we'll see."

After making sure she was safely ensconced in her room at the Reagan House, Slade joined Crane and first they gave the latest addition to the floor decorations a careful examination.

"Not so much money as the last bunch," the sheriff remarked after emptying the pockets. "Guess losing out on good hauls is beginning to hurt."

"Which will mean added activity on the part of the remainder of the bunch," Slade replied. "Which also means we will have to be on our toes. Yes, we can expect more trouble and soon."

"You'll take care of it," Crane predicted cheerfully. "Been doing a very good job so far. Where would you say the hellions are from?"

"New Mexico, eastern Arizona, possibly Oklahoma," was Slade's decision. "Former cowhands who haven't done range work for quite a while."

"Oklahoma," the sheriff repeated. "Texas Panhandle butts right against Oklahoma."

"Yes, it does," Slade admitted with a slight smile, for he had a very good notion what the oldtimer was thinking. Every newcomer was to be regarded sideways until he had proven himself. And Van Rice, the Bar M owner, was a newcomer. Also he was tall and broad, the description of the apparent leader of the outlaw bunch. Yes, the sheriff was quite likely developing notions. Well, that could be passed up for the present.

For some time they discussed things in general, endeavoring to pinpoint where the outlaws might be expected to strike next, with scant success. There were so many things, from express cars to rumholes. Stage coaches and cattle must also be given consideration.

"Well, perhaps something will break for us and give us a lead," Slade said.

"More likely you'll make it break," predicted Crane. "I'm expecting that to happen any day. Any hour, for that matter. Your hunches just drop out of the blue or the thin air."

"Nice to have you feel that way," Slade smiled. "Hope you are right."

"Ain't in the habit of being wrong," the sheriff answered. "Wait till I fetch some coffee from the stove in the back room; it's simmering. That always seems to help, especially when spiked from my bottle. Be right with you."

The coffee was fetched in short order and both felt better after drinking it, the sheriff's well spiked.

"Well, guess we might as well amble back to the Branding Pen," Slade said as Crane rinsed the cups. "Can't see as there is anything else we can do here."

"Yep, guess we might as well," agreed the sheriff, with a complacent glance at his well decorated floor. "Old Doc, the coroner, will want to hold an inquest on those carcasses about tomorrow, when he gets back from Echo."

Looking up, and with a final glance at the bodies, they set out.

"Hello, look who's with us!" the sheriff exclaimed as they entered the Branding Pen. "There's Lance Messa, the builder, talking with Hardrock. Looks dusty, as if he's been riding."

"If he came from Echo, he doubtless has been," Slade agreed, regarding the builder with interest.

"Understand he hopes to tie onto a building contract here," Crane remarked. "An up and coming gent, all right." Slade conceded that he very likely was.

Mary came bouncing in, gay and animated. She had changed to her dancing costume.

"Yes, I want several numbers tonight," she told Slade. "After what happened, I need them." Which Slade thought was not unreasonable.

"Looks like it's not going to rain after all," she said. "Stars are shining brightly. I hope it stays clear; I'd like to get a lot of loading done before night. All right, Walt, let's go. There comes a waltz." They moved onto the floor.

60

They did several numbers, the last a fast one that left Mary rosy and breathless, her eyes sparkling.

"But I feel a lot better," she declared. "Now I figure to be able to sleep tonight."

"Hmmm," said the sheriff. Mary ignored him.

Lance Messa, the builder, walked out, nodding shortly to the sheriff. Crane watched him pass through the swinging doors.

"Jigger don't look to be in as good a temper as usual," he remarked.

"Perhaps one of his building deals isn't turning out too well," Mary ventured. "Lots of competition in that field."

Slade nodded, but did not otherwise comment. His eyes were thoughtful. Which Mary at once noted. However, she said nothing except that she was about ready for the floor again.

The time jogged along, pleasantly enough. Finally Mary glanced at the clock, nodded to Saxon. He spoke to his whoopers and they trooped out, shouting their goodbyes to everybody. A little later Slade and the sheriff and Mary also said goodnight. Crane headed for home, Slade and Mary for the Reagan House, where the old desk clerk smiled benignly as they mounted the stairs together.

CHAPTER
NINE

The following afternoon, Slade and the sheriff resumed their never ending discussion of outlaw antics, arriving at no satisfactory conclusions.

That something was in the works, Slade was convinced. Something that might well mean the death of an innocent person. Which gave him grave concern. His chore, as he saw it, was to prevent such a tragedy. How? He didn't know but was determined to concentrate on the matter until a solution to the problem took form in his mind. And he would have a hunch to that effect.

The sheriff watched him mostly in silence. Slade would talk when ready, not before. Finally he did speak.

"I'm going to take a walk," he said. "That sometimes helps, and at least I can always think better in the open air. I'll drop over to the cart station and see how Mary is making out with the loading. She's got her sunny day she hoped for and should be making good progress."

"Okay," replied the sheriff. "But watch your step and don't take any loco chances. I figure you ain't thought too well of in certain quarters about now. Doc Cooper, the coroner, figures on possibly holding his inquest on those carcasses later in the day. As I said, watch your step."

Slade promised to do so and strolled out.

It was a bright and beautiful day, with just enough of a breeze to temper the heat. Almost at once he felt his thought processes were clearing up. Coming out had been a wise decision.

His first objective was the cart station where he found the loading chore progressing nicely.

"At this rate we should be able to finish the loading tomorrow morning and perhaps roll for Echo in the afternoon," Mary said. "Are you going to ride with us, dear?"

"I rather think so," Slade replied. "That is if something doesn't occur to change my plans. We'll discuss it when the time comes. Well, so long, I'll be seeing you a little later. Sure, we'll have dinner together at the Branding Pen. By the way, have you seen Estevan?"

"He was wandering around, rather aimlessly, a little while ago," the girl answered. "I don't think he had anything particular on his mind. He didn't ask for you. You can figure him being close by, however. I'll be seeing you, dear."

Leaving the station, Mary's blue eyes following him out of sight, he resumed walking.

Slade proceeded to do a little aimless strolling himself, gradually working his way to the canyon mouth.

For Sanderson sat in a deep canyon, one wall of which rose over the main street. Being a crew change point where repairs were made, it boasted machine shops and large assembly yards.

Slade loved the view from the canyon mouth. Everywhere there were mountains fanging into the sky. The tremendous ranges of the Big Bend, and those of the trans-Pecos area, gleaming in the sunshine, lonely, austere, immutable. One with the eternities, counting time not in years but in eons. Impressing that man is but an insect, the earth a speck hanging in space. But man, a thinking creature, is master of all.

Suddenly he smiled. A certain amusement at himself had entered the picture. Communing with the eternities was uplifting and inspiring, but didn't seem to do much toward solving the problem that, like fog on little cat feet, kept creeping into his train of thought, creeping back and creeping back. He smiled again, and the grim mountains seemed to smile back. He felt better. Maybe they or That Which they bowed to might lend a hand. Had happened much that way in the past. With a last lingering glance at the wastelands he loved, he turned and walked slowly uptown to the sheriff's office, pausing again at the cart station for a few words with Mary.

"Yes, we'll surely be able to roll for Echo right after noon tomorrow," she told him. "The boys are doing a wonderful chore of loading. A big train, too, every available cart pressed into service. The well owners will be greatly pleased. Okay, dear, see you later."

For a few minutes after passing the carts, he paused to gaze at the pulsing flame of the sunset, then continued on his way.

64

"Well, did you tie onto a hunch?" the sheriff asked when he entered the office.

"Nope, not yet," Slade replied. "But I do feel better for my walk. Really believe it is going to speed up my thought processes."

He rolled a cigarette and sat smoking, and sipping the coffee the sheriff fetched. Finally he glanced at the clock.

"Tell you what," he said, "I'm going over to the bank to have a chat with Charley, the president. Will see you after we finish talking and we'll have dinner together at the Branding Pen. Mary will be there."

"Charley has lent us a hand more than once," the sheriff said. "Yep, he's been a big help. Maybe he'll turn up something today. I'll be waiting here for you."

It was well past closing time for the bank, but Slade had no trouble obtaining an audience with the president, an old *amigo*.

Charley sent out for coffee and a drink, then said, "Glad you dropped in, Walt. Was planning to send one of the boys for you. I've got something I think you'll find interesting. You know since we've been working together, I've had the boys keep their eyes and ears open, and they learn things. Here's what one managed to ferret out." He paused to light a cigar, then resumed:

"Ever since it became known that Mr. Dunn plans to run his railroad line in the vicinity of Fort Stockton, there have been dealings between Fort Stockton and Echo, with a lot of money changing hands." Slade nodded, for he knew that to be true.

"A big one has just been consummated," Charley continued. "The really hefty sum of money involved will be sent to Echo via an unscheduled stage. A dead secret, of course, but you know what that means to somebody interested in the transaction and managing to learn about it. Somebody, or several somebodies like the bunch you've been larruping of late. Same old procedure, guard on the seat with the stage driver, more locked in the coach, which has small barred windows, the walls sheathed with boiler iron. Money plumb safe, or so the planners think."

"And a perfect setup for a shrewd owlhoot bunch," Slade interpolated. "Yes, the same old story. Made to order for our horned toads. And if a try for that money is going to be made, I know where the try will have to be made."

"Yes?"

"Yes. For nearly the whole way from Fort Stockton to Echo the trail runs over open rangeland, where the stage is safe. The one exception is a long line of breaks, rugged, heavily brush grown, about three miles to the northwest of Echo, through which the trail runs. There everything favors the outlaws, if they can figure a way to handle the stage, and they have proven themselves exceedingly good at handling difficult matters.

"And," he added whimsically, "I'm developing a hunch that a try for the money is going to be made."

"Fine!" chuckled the president. "Your hunches are always straight ones. When you finish the chore, drop in and give me the details."

They laughed together. Slade finished his coffee and returned to the sheriff's office where he acquainted the highly interested Crane with an account of what passed between him and the president.

"Looks like it might be our big chance to bag the whole nest of sidewinders," Crane said. "When did Charley say the stage will reach Echo?"

"Around midnight tomorrow night," Slade replied.

"And we are riding with the carts right after noon tomorrow," the sheriff nodded. "Should be in Echo in plenty of time to handle the chore."

"Looks that way," Slade conceded. "Well, we might as well go eat."

"A prime notion," applauded Crane. "I hanker for a snort. Figuring on how to bag outlaws always makes me hungry."

When they reached the Branding Pen, they found the carters were already at the bar, whoopin' it up.

"Miss Merril said to tell you she was going to lie down an hour," Saxon reported. They decided to wait for her before ordering.

In less than an hour she trotted in, looking fresh as a daisy, as the sheriff expressed it, and declaring she was starved.

So they had a gay dinner together, the assembled carters doing what they could to keep the saloon from getting stodgy, and doing an outstanding chore of just that.

After eating and enjoying a smoke over coffee, Slade strolled back to the kitchen to have a few words with the cook and his helpers, and to line up Estevan on the morrow's activities, the knife man looking pleased and caressing the haft of his blade. The deputies, Blount and Arbaugh, were also lined up. Then, concluding he had done all he could do for the time being, he returned to the table and relaxed comfortably.

After a while Mary expressed a desire to dance, so they did several numbers on the not-too-crowded floor. However, by the time they left it, there was already plenty of business in the making. Mary abruptly skipped across to the orchestra leader and said a few words to him. Smiling delightedly, he seized a guitar and, bowing low to *El Halcón*, brandished it like a war club. His voice rang out —

"*Señoritas* and *Señores!* Silence, please! The treat great for us is in store. *Capitán* will sing!"

"Okay, Walt, you're elected," chuckled the sheriff.

"Looks that way," Slade conceded. He crossed the platform, accepted the guitar.

A sprightly prelude, the instrument responding to a master's touch, a ringing clash of chords, and Slade's great golden baritone-bass pealed and thundered through the room.

Of the mountains and the plains of Texas, he sang, of her rivers, of her cowboys and *vaqueros*, the plodding herds they tended, food for the cities, as were the crops her farmers raised. The glowing beauty of the rangeland under the sun, its purple mystery under the stars. Of the sweat and toil of the day, the song and good fellowship around the campfire at night. Of the locomotive's clanking siderods and booming exhaust.

Songs that dealt with the prosaic things of everyday life, alchemized into dreams of loveliness by the magic of a great voice. A smiling love song that brought back memories for the dance floor girls and with poignant meaning for the girl who waited.

Again the ringing strings and the crash of chords. The guitar still vibrated to his touch. He handed it back to its owner, flashed the white smile of *El Halcón* to the wildly applauding crowd, and returned to his table. Mary laid her hand on his.

Another hour passed. Estevan glanced out the kitchen door, bowed to *El Halcón* and slipped back out of sight. Mary nodded to Saxon. There was a big day coming up. He spoke to his men and they filed out, whooping their goodnights. Slade and Mary soon followed them.

CHAPTER
TEN

The long cart train, heavily loaded, rolled out of Sanderson. Again it was a sunny day, but there was a slight haze in the sky which could mean anything, weather wise.

Slade was watchful as a matter of habit. He doubted very much that they would meet with trouble on the way. Especially if the outlaws had a serious project in mind, and he believed they did.

The train rolled on, the carters shouting and singing. Mary tried to be gay, but she couldn't dismiss from her mind what was before her, a night of danger for Slade. She told herself there was no sense in worrying about him, that the sheriff was right in maintaining that he always came out on top.

But that was cold comfort. The past was one thing, the present and the future something else again.

The sky haze had deepened slightly. Looked like there would be a fairly dark night. Which Slade felt would be to his advantage. Although, of course, it could also advantage the outlaws. Even with the late moon low in the sky it would not be overly good shooting light.

Finally the smudge that marked Echo came into view, and the drivers quickened the pace. It lacked more than an hour to dark when the trail rolled through the cut and came to rest at the station, to be enthusiastically welcomed by assembled well owners who insisted on lending a hand with what unloading could be accomplished before dark. Lerner was there with his check sheets. He and Mary at once got busy.

After stabling his mustang, Estevan slid into the Diehard kitchen for a gabfest with his *amigos* there. Slade and the sheriff retired to Lerner's quarters to smoke and relax until their late dinner.

"Deputies should be here any time now," Crane said. "They planned to leave Sanderson soon as they helped Doc Cooper hold his inquest on those carcasses, presenting your deposition, which he said would be okay."

"Yes, we'll need the deputies," Slade replied. "Chances are, even with them we'll be outnumbered, but we should make out."

"We will," said Crane cheerfully. "I'm itching to line sights with those horned toads."

The deputies appeared shortly. They stabled their mounts and repaired to the Diehard.

The cook brought in coffee to tide over Slade and the sheriff until they ate at the Diehard. Lerner had told Crane where to find a bottle, so the sheriff enjoyed a little spiking.

With the window panes darkening, Mary arrived, reported that the unloading would easily be completed the next day. She scampered upstairs to clean up a little.

"Little gal's worried, and no wonder," said the sheriff. "I sometimes think that women have the harder chore to handle. A man is so busy trying to keep himself in one piece, and enjoying it, that he has no time to bother about himself. While all the women can do is wait and hope."

"I think you have the right of it," Slade agreed soberly. "Tonight you and I are so absorbed in doing for those hellions that there is no room in our minds for anything else, no time to give our imaginations full play. Well, that's the way with the world and the critters that are supposed to run it." For a while they smoked in silence.

Mary came tripping down the stairs, in her dancing costume, and they set out.

The streets were fairly crowded, the saloons even more so, especially the Diehard, where the carters were doing their best to keep things lively and moving, and succeeding.

The advent of Slade and his party set off whoops of greeting, with a stamping of feet and a banging of glasses on the bar, and insistence that they be allowed to buy a round of drinks.

"Any excuse to make a noise," snorted the sheriff. "You'd think they hadn't seen us for a month instead of a couple of hours."

However, he accepted the invitation to drink. Slade took coffee, Mary a small glass of wine. The carters raised their glasses in salute, and whooped louder than ever.

The deputies were already present, so they all had dinner together, taking their time at it. Mary and Slade danced several numbers. The sheriff communed with some friends at the bar, came back to the table and indulged in a final snort.

Finally Slade glanced at the clock. The kitchen door opened a crack and Estevan peered out. Slade nodded, and the door closed. The knife man would be the first at the place of meeting, Lerner's stable.

"Yes, guess we'd better be moving," Slade said to the others. Mary's hand tightened on his, but all she said was, "Take care of yourselves, all of you."

Slade, Crane and the deputies, Blount and Arbaugh, got up and sauntered out.

A short distance up the street, Slade called a halt for a few moments, while he gazed back the way they had come, and was satisfied that nobody had followed them.

Without incident they reached the stable, where they found Estevan awaiting them. They cinched up and rode north by slightly west, Slade setting a moderate pace, scanning the back trail frequently for a while, then facing to the front.

The sky was still hazy, but the overcast had not appreciably thickened and the stars shone through. The upper edge of the late moon was just appearing above the horizon. Already there was a sheen of wan light creeping across the prairie, plenty to reveal to good eyes as large an object as a horse, especially if that horse was moving, Slade, a trifle uneasily, admitted to himself.

Didn't matter much here on the open rangeland, but nearing the breaks it would be different.

"I figure they will act, if there is something in the works, near where the trail enters the breaks from the north," he told the others. "There the chaparral crowds close to the track, with no chance to turn aside to avoid some obstacle directly in front. Watch out for a tree dropped across the trail, or something of the sort. They might use dynamite — they seem to specialize in that — but I rather doubt it. They would hardly risk an explosion so close to town, where it would very likely be heard. When they consummate the robbery, if they do, their logical escape route is through Echo.

"Of course I could be wrong and they would be at the south edge of the breaks, watching this way. I repeat, I don't think so, but if anybody feels a bullet, please let me know."

This supposedly humorous remark was greeted by snorts and growls, with uneasy glances toward the nearing dark line that was the breaks. Only Estevan smiled grimly, and dropped a hand close to his long blade.

Slade really did not think there was any danger that the owlhoots would be holed up near the south edge of the growth, but he admitted to himself that he did feel a bit easier when they reached the gloom of the stand of chaparral with nothing untoward happening.

"Straight ahead, slowly," he told his companions. "I was right, if they are really around, they are near the north edge. Take it easy, now, with your eyes and ears open. I've a hunch this is going to work out fine."

"Thank Pete for your hunches," the sheriff said prayerfully. "May they ever be right!"

Slowly they moved along, curbing their horses, hoping they would kick no loose stone that would rattle and bang. The line of breaks was quite a bit less than a mile thick. Slade estimated the distance they covered, over and over, slowing Shadow even more. He glanced up at the stars, figuring a particularly bright one shone right above the north edge of the growth, and guided himself by it, finally calling a halt where the brush was a trifle thin, especially to the left.

"Here we leave the horses," he breathed. "Don't dare risk them further. They're all well trained beasts and will stand. Into the brush with them. Then we ease along on foot, through the growth. A bit of a slope to the left here, which should be in our favor. Up a couple of yards, or three. Will give us a clear view of the trail, as much of it as can be seen in this light, which, fortunately, keeps getting a bit stronger. No more talking now, Estevan's hand on my shoulder, the others in line behind him. And if the ball opens, crouch down and shoot fast and straight."

At a pace that would have put an ablebodied snail to shame, the posse crept along, Slade leading, ears attuned to catch any sound, his remarkable eyes searching for any sign of movement.

Abruptly he halted, the others freezing behind him. His sensitive hearing had registered a tiny metallic sound, directly ahead. The jingle of a bit iron as a horse petulantly tossed its head. Then, he was sure, a mutter of low voices.

His hunch was a straight one. The outlaws were here, waiting for the stage to appear. They were but a few paces to the north of where the posse hunkered down.

And then another sound, which quickly the posse also caught, the grind of steel tires on the rocky surface of the trail. The stage from Fort Stockton was rapidly approaching. Slade tensed for instant action. Now he could just make out a shadowy something at the edge of the growth, a clump of horses.

The moon was well up and there was quite a bit more light outlining the trail.

On came the stage, louder and louder. It hove into view, rocking and swaying. It lacked but a few paces of being opposite where the posse crouched when there was a crackling and splintering, and a ponderous thud as the coach plunged into an excavation that spanned the narrow trail from side to side, sagging against the side of the pit. The frenzied lead horses tore free and went racing down the trail. The frantic wheelers were blocked by the side of the pit. The driver and the outside guard were hurled from their seat and into the brush on the opposite side of the hole.

What followed was a hideous pandemonium — the screams of the horses, yells and curses from inside the coach, and a blaze of guns as from the brush charged six horsemen shooting at the sagging vehicle

"Let them have it!" Slade roared as both his big Colts bellowed. The posse guns boomed, Estevan's knife hissed. Almost as if by magic there were three

76

bodies on the ground. Slade fired again, as did the posse, and another outlaw fell. The remaining two still in their saddles, almost hidden by the powder fog, whirled their horses and streaked north, instantly out of sight.

"Hold it!" Slade shouted to the posse, "they're gone."

CHAPTER
ELEVEN

The driver and the outside guard, cut and scratched and bruised, crawled from the brush on the far side of the trail, sputtering profanity. Inside the coach were yells and cursing. Again Slade sent his great voice rolling in thunder —

"Shut up in there! I'll get you out in a minute."

"We can't get out!" a voice wailed. "Door won't open."

With a mutter of disgust, Slade descended to the trail, seized the door handle and tore it open.

"Come out of there, and bring your money pokes with you," he ordered. "If you have a lantern, bring it, too."

"Got one if it isn't busted," came the muffled voice. "Yep, here it is, okay."

The speaker crawled out, followed by two more. All carried stout sacks, plus the lantern one bore.

"Why, hello, Sheriff!" he exclaimed. "And Mr. Slade, ain't it? Heard plenty about you, Mr. Slade, Lots of folks up at Stockton say you're General Manager. Dunn's trouble shooter. Don't know about that, but we're sure glad to be here. You saved a lot of money tonight, but I've a notion that, so far as us fellers are

78

concerned, you saved something money can't buy. Yes, I have a prime notion those devils wouldn't have left us alive after they tied onto a killer bunch." The driver interrupted the garrulous guard.

"How in blazes did they manage to drop us into that hole?" he wondered. "I was watching ahead, close, and didn't see a thing."

"Very smart, but simple," Slade explained. "Excavated the pit — a couple of men with picks and shovels could have completed the chore in short order. Interlaced tree branches over the hole, then canvas on top of the interlacing. Dust sprinkled on the canvas, so it would look no different from the rest of the trail. But when you struck it, down went the coach. Lucky you and your outside guard got pitched into the bushes on the far side of the trail. Otherwise you would have been prime targets from the devils when they came out of the brush on this side, shooting. Well, they'll have to send a crew from Echo to haul the coach out of that hole. The wheelers have quieted down and the others didn't run far. Nor did the cayuses those hellions rode, well trained critters."

By the light of the lantern, he examined the various injuries, decided they were not serious and could wait for treatment until Echo was reached.

He and the sheriff gave the four bodies a brief once-over, plucking off the false beards they wore.

Ornery looking hellions was the concensus of opinion. Slade considered them about average of their brand. A cart would be sent for them. The horses were good animals. Slade was unfamiliar with the brands they bore, although he rather thought a couple were Oklahoma burns that had been slickironed. The four guards, hugging their money pokes, rode them to town. The stage driver had contrived a makeshift bridle for one of the stage horses and would make out for the short ride. The others were stripped of the broken harness and turned loose to graze until picked up. The posse retrieved their mounts and the motley procession got under way.

"Again you planned it just right," the sheriff said to Slade. "We were in the dark, while they were in the moonlight. Was like shootin' settin' quail. Do you figure the head of the pack was one of the pair that got away?"

"That's my opinion," the Ranger replied. "I barely got a glimpse of them, but I'm pretty sure one was big and tall, which none of the bodies are. Yes, his luck held again, if you wish to call it luck rather than hairtrigger thinking. Well, maybe next time."

"Yep, just a matter of time," said Crane. "Anyhow, we didn't do too bad, saved the money, and did for four of the hellions."

"And my blade did not thirst," Estevan murmured.

Slade decided the Diehard would be the first stop. There the aid of the carters could be enlisted.

It was not so very late and they collected quite an entourage as they passed through the streets. But at the Diehard, the carters took care of matters. Very quickly, two carts went roaring to the breaks to pick up the bodies and place them in Lerner's stable.

In the Diehard back room, Slade, with Mary assisting, took care of the stage crew's minor injuries.

The money pokes were locked in the Diehard safe, along with the head guard's tally sheets and other documents. It would be apportioned the following afternoon.

Lerner had already made arrangements to have the coach lifted from the excavation, come daylight. Quarters for the stage crew had been reserved, and after a few drinks they went to bed.

"Some of the boys were getting badly worried when that stage didn't show up," Lerner said. "I told them not to worry and hope for the best."

"That must have made them feel a lot better," snorted the sheriff. "Waiter!" Lerner grinned at Slade and sampled his drink. Mary frowned at both of them.

"What a reprehensible sense of humor," she scolded. "I can sympathize with those poor men. Waiting and waiting for something or somebody is no fun."

"Guess you should know," said the sheriff. "Fact is I get a little taste of it myself now and then."

The cart loaded with the bodies rolled in, the carters whooping blithely.

"Listen to them!" said their scandalized employer. "You'd think they were returning from a picnic."

"Was a picnic for them," was Crane's cheerful rejoinder. "For all honest men, for that matter. Here's hoping there will be more of the same."

Mary did not argue that. Instead she said, "Come on, Walt, one more dance before closing time."

Slade was agreeable and they made it two.

"I've also already arranged for the bodies to be headed for town early," Lerner said. "Deputy Blount says he will go along if it is okay with you, Tom."

"That's good," replied Crane. "Will give Sanderson folks a chance to look them over, and we should get rid of them soon after the cart train rolls in next day. Much obliged, Westbrook, you always do the right thing."

"I'm sometimes not sure," the oil magnate differed. "We can't all be like Walt."

Miss Merrill sniffed daintily, but patted Slade's hand.

"I'll give the boys another hour to get over the excitement," she said. "We'll have an easy chore finishing the unloading before night. Let them have a little fun when they have the chance."

"My sentiments," said the sheriff. Slade and Lerner also thought it a good idea, as did Deputy Arbaugh, who would sleep at Rader's place.

"One nice thing about being a bachelor," the owner said. "Always plenty of room."

"Sometimes," Miss Merril observed dryly. The sheriff shook with laughter.

The carters took full advantage of their additional hour and proceeded to liven things up, decidedly.

Finally, Mary nodded to Saxon, who led his vociferous charges out, probably to the relief of citizens of the neighborhood.

Estevan peered from the kitchen, bowed to *El Halcón* and slipped back out of view. Mary and Slade said goodnight to the sheriff and Rader, and walked slowly to the Reagan House.

CHAPTER
TWELVE

The following afternoon found Slade and the sheriff back at the good old guessing game, which dealt with the possible, even probable doings of the outlaws. Neither expected undue activity for the day or the following night, but experience had taught them to be ever vigilant; it was an almost unpredictable bunch.

"And the hellions must be in a temper for fair," observed Crane. "There was a small fortune in those three pokes they didn't tie onto."

"Yes, and they will sure be out to even the score as soon as they figure they have a chance to," Slade said. "We can look for trouble very soon."

"Guess you'll take care of any they manage to shove out," replied the sheriff.

Lerner dropped in. "While the boys are having a snack and a breather, I moseyed up through the cut for a look at the machine shop and the assembly yard," he explained. "Ran into Messa, the builder. He was looking things over, too. Expect he has an eye out for possible business. Got to talking. He asked a lot of questions about the oil field, drills, and so forth. Seems to know quite a bit about them."

"Not unreasonable to believe he does, seeing as where he appears to be concentrating his efforts," Slade said.

"Guess that's so," Lerner agreed. "Well, I'm going back to the station to give Mary a hand with the unloading. Coming down after a while?"

"Chances are we will," Slade answered. Lerner ambled out. The sheriff shot *El Halcón* a speculative glance, but asked no questions, and charged his pipe in silence.

Slade rolled a cigarette and also smoked in silence, gazing thoughtfully out the window at the sun glow.

Says the "book" of the Rangers, not a book of the printed page but of the annals of experience:

"Find the motive and you are well on the way to corraling your man."

And *El Halcón* believed he had finally discovered the motive, the reason for the intense activities of the outlaws. They, or at least the head man, had something in mind far more lucrative than robbery and burgling, or so he thought.

Later Slade would discuss the matter with Lerner and the sheriff. Not, perhaps, until he had amassed a little more corroborative evidence against the gentleman in question.

"Let's go down to the cart station and see how the unloading is coming along," he suggested.

"Suits me," answered Crane. "It's nice out. Let's go."

They locked up and departed, strolling slowly through the warm sunshine.

84

Such a town as Echo habitually boasted plenty of saloons, but it seemed there was always room for one more, which the sheriff commented on. "Feller named Bloodshaw opened up a new one over close to the oil field," he remarked. "Calls it the Easy Rest. 'Pears to be doing all right, too. Gets lots of the field workers, and those jiggers make good money and like to spend. Like to have a look at the place?"

"Not a bad idea," Slade conceded. They turned toward the field.

"There it is," Crane said, after they had walked a little ways and were nearing the field.

"Tightly built little house," Slade commented.

"Laid out well inside, too," replied the sheriff. "Between the barroom and the back room is a little cubbyhole where the stock is kept. If the bartender needs to replenish stock he can get it without bothering the owner working in the back room."

Slade regarded the Easy Rest with interest.

"Who erected it?" he asked.

"Our *amigo*, the builder, Lance Messa," the sheriff answered.

"I see," Slade said thoughtfully.

Peering through the plate glass window, they saw the long bar was pretty well lined with oil field workers and others. However, they decided not to enter but continued to the cart station.

There they found the unloading almost completed, Mary and Lerner busy with their check lists.

"Be finished by dark and be all set to roll for Sanderson in the morning," the girl told them. "I'll rest

85

for a while and join you at the Diehard for dinner. Been peaceful here all day, and I hope it stays that way during the night. I can use a really peaceful night for a change. Be seeing you."

Slade and the sheriff continued their stroll, mostly in silence, each busy with his thoughts. They walked to the canyon mouth and watched the glory of the sunset. With the flame-tipped hues fading and the stars taking over, they returned to Lerner's quarters to wait for Mary who appeared before long.

They enjoyed a quiet dinner, danced a few numbers, chatted a while. Mary got her peaceful night.

Before mid morning, the empties rolled for Sanderson. With them rode Slade, the sheriff, Deputy Blount, and Estevan. Deputy Arbaugh would remain in Echo for a couple of days to keep an eye on things there.

He would be needed.

Slade was more than usually watchful, for with frustrated outlaws plus Saxon's plump money poke, anything could be expected. He and Estevan scouted ahead and when they reached the first line of breaks, their horses were moving at little better than a walk, with Slade scanning every stand of thicket, watching for moving sapling tops that would indicate the passage of mounted men. No act of bird or little beast escaped his carping gaze. He correctly interpreted their notes of song or whimpering cries. Anything that seemed in the least out of the ordinary was studied with eyes that did not make mistakes.

Through the first line of breaks with nothing untoward happening, as Slade really believed would be the case. However, he was not going to allow himself to be lulled into a sense of false security. There were three more breaks ahead, each with its own particular threat.

The second line of breaks was passed without incident. The same applied to the third. And now ahead was the crucial test, the fourth line, close to town, an escape route provided, where already an unsuccessful attempt had been made. Even in the still bright sunlight the long bristle of growth looked dark and ominous. Were anything to happen, there was where it would be. Slade tensed for instant action. Estevan dropped a hand to his long throwing knife, his black eyes snapping.

Into the shadows they went, their attention focused on the winding trail ahead and the slopes on either side. It didn't seem possible that the outlaws would make a try for the heavily guarded train, which they must know was very much on the alert; but they might figure a way.

And though he was fairly certain they would not meet with trouble, he admitted to himself that he drew a breath of relief when the last cart rolled from the growth and onto the open prairie. Now just a routine roll to Sanderson, with Mary declaring she was starved and the sheriff demanding a snort without delay as the dying sunlight glinted on bit and bridle iron.

With the full dark closing down, the lights of the railroad town glittered in the distance, and soon the train was rumbling through the streets to the cart station, with rest and oats in the offing for the weary horses and food and drink for their drivers and riders.

Word of the foiled stage robbery had reached Sanderson and the carters were soon putting forth their version of the affair. Which if it lacked in accuracy made up in enthusiasm.

Hardrock sat at the table with Slade and his companions to make sure they'd be allowed to enjoy their very late dinner in peace. Estevan was regaling the kitchen force with his version of the happening, and relaying to his *amigos* certain instructions Slade had given him. Instructions that would have greatly surprised anybody but the knife man, whom nothing ever surprised. If *Capitán* said a thing was so, it was so.

Lively and pleasant hours followed. But there was plenty of loading work ahead the following morning and it was decided to make it a fairly early night.

Meanwhile the outlaws were not idle. Slade later insisted he had been outsmarted, although the sheriff differed with him on that score.

CHAPTER
THIRTEEN

Bloodshaw, the Easy Rest Saloon owner, was a genial host and well liked by his patrons, a good tempered but noisy crowd, and there had been no trouble worthy of the name in the Easy Rest.

Bloodshaw, the doors locked, the barred windows closed, sat in the rear room tabulating the week's take, no small sum, that he planned to send via train to the Sanderson bank the following day. He looked up at a sound behind him and saw four bearded men, one tall and broad, looming over him. He instinctively made a grab for something in his desk drawer, which was a mistake. A gun barrel thudded against his head and stretched him bleeding and stunned on the floor.

The tall robber scooped the money on the table into a sack and all four glided into the little cubbyhole room next to the barroom, and out of sight.

Bloodshaw, suffering from but a minor injury, regained consciousness, scrambled and lurched to his feet and ran into the barroom, shouting what happened, to the accompaniment of plenty of noise and sympathy.

How the robbers got in was a question. Bloodshaw insisted they must have slipped in from the barroom. The head bartender was positive they did not.

The outer door was examined and found to be locked and barred. They certainly didn't get in that way. Nor by way of the barred windows, which were also examined.

Somebody recalled that Deputy Arbaugh was in the Diehard, or had been, although Sheriff Crane had departed early in the afternoon and by now must be in Sanderson. It was decided to notify the deputy at once, although it was admitted that very likely there was nothing he could do other than send the sheriff a wire.

Arbaugh was contacted. It was not so very late and he decided on a little personal investigation before sending the wire, and visited the Easy Rest, and learned nothing more than what he had been told.

The theory was advanced that somehow the robbers had hidden themselves in the shadowy cubbyhole room until Bloodshaw opened his safe and took the money out.

An explanation that was preposterous, for there was nothing in the little room behind which they could have hidden.

"Just wait till Mr. Slade gets here day after tomorrow," said Arbaugh. "I'll guarantee he figures it out." To which there was general agreement.

The head bartender was an experienced oldtimer and quickly took care of Bloodshaw's gashed scalp, opining the wound was of no consequence and advising the owner to go to bed and forget about it.

Arbaugh sent the wire, a laconic, "Easy Rest robbed," and returned to the Diehard for a little refreshment after his labors.

Slade and the others were getting ready to call it a night when the wire arrived. The sheriff swore. Slade looked very thoughtful. Estevan smiled, and caressed the haft of his knife.

Mary also was thoughtful, but duly thankful no activity at the moment was involved.

"Let's get out of here before something does happen," she said. Which was taken as sound advice.

Doc Cooper held his inquest. The undertaker removed the bodies. Sheriff Crane eyed the bare floor with disapproval.

"But won't be that way long," he predicted. "All set for the next batch."

No further word concerning the robbery of the Easy Rest came from Echo, which was as expected.

"We'll get the details, if there are any to get, when the loaded carts roll into Echo tomorrow," Slade said. "And anyhow, I am willing to wager that Messa is mixed up in it somehow."

"You've got that hellion tagged as head of the pack, ain't you?" commented the sheriff. "You got me looking sideways at him a few days back. Guess I'm getting smart — figuring things out for myself a mite."

"Yes, Lance Messa is the head man," Slade agreed.

"And how did you get the lowdown on him?"

"He is smart, able, with a quick mind and even quicker action, but he makes the little slips that his brand seem always prone to make." Slade replied. "Very quickly it became obvious that he was keeping tabs on me and my movements. That, of course, set me thinking. That stupid attempt to drygulch me from the basin crest when I rode into Echo instantly told me that somebody regarded me as a menace that should be removed as quickly as possible. My *El Halcón* repute goes ahead of me and Messa at once decided I was a threat to the success of the complicated plan he had evolved that, did he manage to put it over, would pay off tremendously. Of course, I had no idea at the time who was the individual so anxious to get rid of me, or why, but I at once began studying everybody who could possibly fit into the role. Didn't take long to narrow down the real suspects. I had become convinced that it was a newcomer to the section. I decided it must be either Messa or Van Rice, and it didn't take long to eliminate Rice."

"The jigger I had been sorta puzzled about for a while," interpolated the sheriff.

"Very quickly, Rice faded out of the picture," Slade said. "I knew he didn't have the knowledge to even understand vaguely the scheme that somebody had evolved, dealing as it did with the great oil pool to the north of Echo and the modern machinery that might make it possible to tap the pool. I believe it could be done, but as I told Lerner and Dunn, it would require a very large outlay of capital Messa didn't have but was trying desperately to amass by his robberies and burgling. There was the motive it was so necessary to learn.

"As for Messa, his standing as a competent builder put him in a position to learn things not generally known, such as the money stage from Fort Stockton.

"But it seemed that very frequently the buildings he erected were getting into mixups of one sort or another. For instance, the attempt to rob the well owner by dropping him and his two guards into a hole right in front of the structure he was building, with undoubtedly knowledge of the building and its environs.

"Messa's Mexican builders don't talk. They may wonder about things, but they don't talk about them, shrugging them off as no concern of theirs in which they are right. They get well paid for their work, and that's all they are interested in. Well, have you had enough for the time being?"

"Yep, plenty to hold me," replied the sheriff. "You make out a prime Judge Colt case against the devil. Just a matter of time."

"Hope you're right," Slade said. "One thing I'd like to know for sure."

"What's that?"

"Van Rice's real attitude toward the railroad, which of course I'll have to learn."

"Oh, you will," nodded Crane. "And you'll swing him in line for Mr. Dunn. No doubt in my mind about that, either. But how do you feel about Rice's attitude toward Messa's planning to drill wells on his land?"

"I'd say Rice would be glad to sell or lease any land Messa might want, not caring what he would do with it. Like most cowmen, he doesn't have any use for oil wells but knows there is no stopping them.

"Not that Messa will ever have a chance to drill a well," he concluded grimly. "We'll take care of that."

"You're darn right," growled the sheriff. "Well, shall we amble down and see how the loading is coming along?"

"Not a bad idea," Slade agreed. "I think Mary is pretty sure she'll get it all done before dark and be ready to roll in the morning. Hope so, I'm curious about the Easy Rest affair. The quicker we get back to Echo the better I'll be pleased." Crane locked the door and they set out.

"Guess the devils made a good haul last night," he remarked.

"Logical to think so," Slade answered. "Bloodshaw is new to the section and is liable to be a bit careless. Expect he had a week's take exposed. Last night may teach him to be more careful, though it seems some folks will never learn."

Reaching the station, they found Mary busy, the loading going along at a fast pace.

"Sure we'll roll in the morning," she said. "We'll be finished with the loading before dark. The boys are working like beavers. They are anxious to get back to the Diehard. They've taken a great liking to the place. The very pretty dance floor girls may have something to do with that. I think Walt is anxious to get back, too. He figures he has a better chance to get into trouble in Echo than he has in Sanderson. Okay, I'll see you later. We'll have dinner together in the Branding Pen."

Slade and the sheriff agreed that would be a good idea and they continued their stroll.

They intercepted Estevan near the mouth of the canyon. He chatted with them a little, but had nothing

94

of interest to report. Once again they watched the sunset which had a never failing fascination, then walked back to the office to relax a little before eating.

For a while they indulged in the guessing game. Question: where would the outlaws strike next. Slade felt it would be Tumble or Echo, not Sanderson, although he knew he could be wrong.

Finally they gave it up, joined Mary in the Branding Pen and partook of their evening meal.

It had been a long, hard day and even the carters were a bit subdued. Again an early night was in order.

CHAPTER
FOURTEEN

They were not subdued the following morning, with the long train of carts rolling through the golden sunshine. The birds in the thickets were hard put to keep up with their caterwauling.

The first line of breaks was passed through. Slade was watchful during the passage, but not apprehensive. He felt almost sure for certain that no attempt of any kind would be made against the train. But with such a character as Lance Messa, he was taking no chances. No telling what might be cooking up in that unusual brain of his.

The second line of breaks was a repeat, as were the third and the fourth. Soon the smoke smudge of Echo stained the sky, and there still remained nearly three hours of sunlight when the train rolled through the cut and came to rest beside the station.

Lerner was there with his check sheets, and present also were a number of oil field workers to help with the unloading. The cart crew took time for a drink and a snack and then went to work, singing and shouting. It had been a really pleasant run, with an even pleasanter night in the offing.

The oil magnate insisted that Mary trot up to his quarters to rest and clean up a bit; he and Saxon would take care of everything until she returned. Slade and the sheriff walked with her and made themselves comfortable, sipping coffee the cook brought them, and smoking. When Mary came back downstairs they escorted her to the carts.

"And now what?" the sheriff asked.

"Now," Slade replied, "I wish to have a look at the Easy Rest saloon, the saloon that was robbed.

The sheriff led the way. Although it was still early, the place was already doing some business. He and Bloodshaw, the owner were acquainted. Bloodshaw, his head bandaged, shook hands warmly with Slade. He rehashed the details of the robbery, as well as he knew them.

"The big mystery," he said, "is how did the devils get in? I still say they slipped in from the barroom when nobody was looking and slipped out the same way. My head bartender swears they didn't. Stalemate, Mr. Slade. Maybe you can solve the mystery. Judging from what Tom has told me about you, I've a strong notion that you can. What's the first move?"

"First I wish to look at that cubbyhole room you spoke of. Fetch a good strong light." Bloodshaw procured a suitable lamp and led the way into the cubbyhole.

"Want the door shut? Bloodshaw asked.

"And locked," Slade replied. "Also the door to the outside. Just possible we may uncover something you will prefer not to be generally known. I know all this sounds melodramatic, sir, but I'll explain the reason later."

Taking the lamp, Slade went over the little room, foot by foot. First he examined the floor, and discovered nothing. Next he gave his attention to the walls.

There were shelves nailed and bracketed to the inner wall, to accommodate stock. The opposite wall, which faced the outside of the building, was paneled. Slade gave the paneling meticulous care. Suddenly he uttered a low exclamation.

First he had noted that the panels were of different thickness, some slightly elevated above the adjoining ones. Then he saw what only the keenest eyes would have noticed.

Scoring a panel was an indenture, the little notches so tiny as to be almost invisible. It followed three sides of the panel, a vertical scoring from close to the floor to a height of slightly more than five feet, two transverse scorings, one close to the floor, the other joining the crest of the vertical indenture. The length of the transverse scorings were about four feet.

The indentures were no thicker than the thickness of a fingernail.

Slade inserted a fingernail into the vertical indenture, exerted a little pressure. The panel slid back noiselessly on sanded and oiled surfaces to reveal an opening plenty large enough to admit a stooping man. It also revealed the outer sheathing scored by lines of indentures. A nail inserted and the sheathing began moving. Slade stopped it with a lateral pressure of his palm and the slight opening closed. A similar procedure

98

with the inner panel and it also closed, leaving only the blank inner wall. Slade turned to his astounded companions.

"See how they got in and out?" he asked. "Very simple, very shrewd, and a masterpiece of cabinet work."

"Well, I'll be a sheepherder's uncle!" said Bloodshaw.

"The blankety-blank sidewinders!" said the sheriff.

Slade chuckled, but was immediately grave.

"Mr. Bloodshaw," he said, "I seriously request you don't mention this to anybody. By not doing so, you may well help bring the miscreants to justice. Without delay, have the shelves similar to those on the inner wall nailed and bracketed onto this wall, over the panel, so it can't be opened, against the possibility of an attempted repeat performance. Putting up the shelves will occasion no comment — you need them for stock."

"I'll take care of it right away," Bloodshaw promised. "And Mr. Slade, you can depend on me to cooperate in every way to the fullest extent. And thank you, very, very much for everything, Sheriff, you're lucky to have such a man working with you."

"Don't I know it!" growled Crane. "Just a matter of time until he drops a loop on the devils." Slade deftly created a diversion —

"Tom, I think we should drop back to the cart station and see how the unloading is coming along."

"That's right," agreed the sheriff. "Be seeing you, Bloodshaw."

"And again thank you both for everything," repeated the Easy Rest owner.

As they walked back to the cart station, the sheriff suddenly remarked, "He was so excited he didn't wonder who was responsible for that contraption."

"I endeavored to steer the conversation away from it," Slade replied. "He doesn't need to know about Messa. The fewer persons know what we know the better."

"My sentiments," said Crane. "Do you believe he has caught on that we have the lowdown on him?"

"I don't think he has," Slade said. "He is undoubtedly an egoist and thinks he has everybody fooled."

"He did have everybody fooled except *El Halcón*," insisted the sheriff.

"It is possible," Slade conceded. "But not everybody was on the lookout for somebody who might fill the bill."

Crane grunted and did not argue the point further.

Reaching the cart station, they found everything in order, the unloading proceeding apace. The carters whooped greetings. The oil field workers grinned and bobbed.

Mary favored them with a suspicious glance, but was apparently satisfied with their expressions, for she indulged in no scoldings.

"I'm fine," she replied to Slade's question as to how she was making out. "That is if I don't topple over from hunger. I didn't put away much of the snack, and now I'm beginning to feel that was a mistake. Well, we'll eat dinner at the Diehard by dark. Guess I can hold off until then. Better for my figure anyhow, a little holding off."

100

"Any improvement would be devastating, where the onlooker is concerned," Lerner declared gallantly.

"Sounds nice," Mary admitted. "But did you notice that sarcastic gleam in Uncle Tom's eye? To say nothing of the amused one in Walt's."

"And he should be able to figure the right or the wrong of it," said the sheriff.

"And I think this discussion has gone long enough," Miss Merril said. "Besides, I've got work to do. See you at dinner." She went back to her check lists. Slade and the sheriff resumed their stroll.

They walked slowly, enjoying the bracing air, making their way toward the north slope of the basin, liking the play of lights and shadows on the rim of the bowl. For it was nearing sunset.

"There's the old Wallop Saloon you'll have reason to remember," the sheriff remarked. "Looks better than it used to, don't you think?" Slade nodded and studied the building for a few moments.

CHAPTER
FIFTEEN

The Wallop was a saloon that was constantly changing hands. It had been opened up by Frederick Norton, the notorious outlaw who lost a gun battle with Walt Slade. Next a gentleman named Vandyke took over and made a go of it. Now it was owned by one Simon Hoskins, new to the section. He was up and coming and made a lot of improvements, enlarging the building, putting in better furnishings. He did an excellent business, getting cowhands from the north, oil field workers, and railroaders. The place was noisy but experienced little serious trouble.

Back of the Wallop was a narrow alley with a straggle of growth along the far side.

Slade and the sheriff continued walking until they reached the breakthrough, out of which the workers were streaming. They shouted greetings and hurried along, doubtless with visions of food and drink awaiting them.

"Guess we'd better head back down," said the sheriff. "Be dark before we reach the Diehard. Mustn't keep the hungry gal waiting."

It was dark before they reached the Diehard, where the carters were already whooping it up. Mary and

Lerner had retired to his quarters to give the girl a chance to clean up and change before eating.

They arrived shortly, Mary voicing her hungry plaint. Rader, the owner, hurried to the kitchen.

"Everything went along smoothly," Mary said. "Unloading finished on time, the well owners pleased and clamoring for more. We can roll for Sanderson with the empties tomorrow. Money paid over — Mr. Rader has it locked up in his safe. Estevan? I think he is scouting around. We saw him as we came down but didn't get a chance to speak with him. He was headed north and walking rather fast. Will they never get here with something to eat! I'm famishing."

In due time the cook came through in fine style and his culinary offerings were fully appreciated. After which was a comfortable period of relaxation with smokes, and a glass of wine for Mary.

Estevan had still not put in an appearance and Slade began to wonder a little. Began to look like the knife man might have hit on something.

Slade and Mary danced several numbers. She also danced with Lerner and Saxon. Deputy Arbaugh came in and accepted a chair and a drink.

Estevan appeared with startling suddenness, his eyes glittering. He came straight to the table and spoke, his voice hardly above a whisper.

"*Capitán*," he said, "in the alley behind the Wallop Saloon stand the *ladrón* and four other *hombres* whose look I liked not. They at the edge of the brush stand and the back door of the saloon they watch. What does *Capitán* think?"

"I think," Slade said, rising to his feet, "that we'd better be getting up there as fast as we can. Be lucky if we're not already too late. Come on, Arbaugh."

He waved to the dance floor and the anxious-eyed girl there and sauntered out, the others close behind him.

Outside, he quickened his pace, making sure with a couple of glances that nobody was following them.

Straight across town to the north slope of the basin the posse sped, the sheriff and the deputy breathing hard before they reached their destination.

"We'll enter the alley from the east and hug the straggle of brush until we are close to the Wallop's back door," Slade said. "Easy now, take it slow, and try not to make a sound. I think we are in time, from the noise in the saloon. The devils must be waiting for some kind of signal before making a move. No more talking now, and be ready for business."

With Slade leading, they entered the narrow and dark alley, crowding against the brush, easing ahead at a creeping pace. They were not far from being opposite the Wallop's back door when Slade halted, the others close behind him. He had spotted the dark clump he knew to be the waiting outlaws. Motionless, straining eyes and ears! Inside the saloon sounded the usual cheerful racket. No alarm there, so far.

And then abruptly, there was plenty of alarm. The posse jumped as from inside the Wallop came a crackling stutter of gunfire, and a wild yelling.

From the brush dashed five bearded men, one tall and broad. He hit the door with a big shoulder and it

104

slammed open. Inside streamed the outlaws with, they didn't know it, the posse close on their heels.

Slade also hit the sagging door. It flew wide, revealing just what he expected. Hoskins, the owner, was rising from a table covered with money the big man was preparing to rake into a sack. Close to him and not far from the barroom door were four more bearded men with guns trained on Hoskins.

Slade's great voice rolled through the barroom tumult — "Up! You are under arrest!"

The robbers spun around as if on pivots. The room rocked to the blaze of gunfire that dwarfed that in the barroom.

Two of the outlaws fell as Slade's Colts boomed, the reports echoed by the posse's guns. Estevan's knife hissed and a third was down. The remaining two, one the big man with whom Slade vainly tried to line sights, his companion shielding him, went racing through the barroom door and into the madhouse crowd there, Slade bounding in pursuit, dodging past the bodies and the overturned table. He saw his man, almost at the swinging doors, but dared not shoot lest he kill somebody other than his quarry whom he was sure was Lance Messa. And by the time he had torn through the crowd, flinging men right and left, and reached the swinging doors, there was nobody in sight. With a disgusted mutter, he holstered his guns and let loose a roar that restored something like order, he being at once recognized.

"What happened out here?" he asked the head bartender.

"Hardly know, Mr. Slade," The drunk juggler replied, "A couple of crazy galoots by the door commenced shooting holes in the ceiling and the walls. Didn't hit anybody, but scared the blazes out of us — no telling where those slugs might land. When the hell cut loose in the back room, they ran out."

"An old owlhoot trick, but effective," Slade said. "Create a diversion elsewhere to hold everybody's attention while the outlaws do their work. Better send your waiters and floor men in to collect the money on the floor. The table covered with it got knocked over."

When he returned to the back room, Slade found the sheriff complacently regarding the scene of carnage.

"Not bad," he said. "Did for three of the sidewinders and saved Hoskins' money. I gave him a good scolding for having a full week's take layin' around to tempt the owlhoots. He promised to do better. Like most newcomers to the section, he was inclined to discount the stories he heard. Guess he won't again. Nope, not a bad night's work."

"But the one I was most anxious to account for escaped, per usual," Slade said wearily. "Oh, well, perhaps next time; I'm getting heartily tired of saying that."

"Just a matter of time," was the cheerful rejoinder.

The table had been set on its legs again, the scattered money, or all but a few stray coins, had been recovered. And now the place was packed, for the shooting had been heard and people were coming from every direction.

106

Estevan had raced down to the Diehard to allay the anxiety there. He returned, Mary and Lerner accompanying him.

"Same old story," the girl said. "Out of my sight a minute and you're into something."

"Sort of had this one forced on me," Slade defended his actions. Miss Merril did not seem overly impressed.

"I'm hungry," she said.

"And I crave a snort," added the sheriff.

"Okay," Slade said. "We'll give the bodies a quick once-over, and then the Diehard."

A brief examination of the bodies revealed nothing that Slade considered significant. They were dressed in rangeland garments, but the condition of their hands indicated they had not done work of any kind for quite a while. The false beards were removed and everybody allowed to take a look. The Wallop bartender was sure he had seen at least two of them at the bar earlier in the evening.

"Looking the place over, eh?" remarked the sheriff.

"I'll have some of the boys pack them to the stable," Lerner offered.

"That will be good," Slade accepted. "Tomorrow we'll load them into the carts rolling to Sanderson. All right, everybody? Let's go."

Before they left, Hoskins insisted on shaking hands with Slade and thanked him profusely for everything.

"Estevan, how did you happen to spot those devils lurking in the alley like you did?" Slade asked.

"Their looks I liked not and when they walked up the street as if business on, I followed," was the laconic response. "The beards they wore not, and with them the *ladrón*, Messa walked not. He them joined in the alley."

"I see," Slade said smilingly. "Well, you did a mighty good chore." Estevan bowed low.

"To be by *El Halcón* praised is the honor great," he murmured.

The sheriff wondered if Messa had anything to do with the new construction work done on the Wallop building. Lerner thought not but conceded that he had probably looked it over, there being nothing unusual about one builder studying another's project.

"If he'd had a hand in it, very likely we would have run into something more complicated," Slade said.

"Well, anyway we can chalk up one for our side," said Crane. "Sort of evens up for the Bloodshaw affair the hellions put over."

Without further misadventure, they reached the Diehard, the carters whooping a greeting. Some of them had visited the Wallop and were spreading their own version of the affair, which was startling to say the least.

Slade and his companions settled down to a period of comfortable relaxation which they felt they could use. Mary got her snack, the others liquid refreshment, including coffee for Slade. Estevan drifted to the kitchen to eat and drink with his friends there.

Mary and Slade had a few dances together, but it was getting late, with a hard day in the offing. Everybody called it an early night.

108

CHAPTER
SIXTEEN

An hour or so before mid morning, Slade and Mary ate breakfast together.

"I was afraid the nice weather wouldn't continue much longer," Mary said gazing disapprovingly out the window at the gloomy prospect. "No golden sunshine and blue skies today. Oh well, take it as it comes and don't complain. Were there never any clouds, we wouldn't appreciate the sunshine."

"That's the right attitude," Slade approved. "Will be nice and cool, too, which is something. Was just a mite warm yesterday."

"Enough snorts of redeye and everything is rosy," opined the sheriff. "Let us drink!"

Under the gray sky, the carts rolled for Sanderson, the bodies of the slain outlaws reposing supinely in one. With the train rode Slade, Estevan and the sheriff. Deputy Arbaugh would remain in Echo a couple more days.

The air was very cool and slickers were donned against probable rain.

Walt Slade was forced to admit he liked such days. When mountains seemed taller, rivers broader, and the wind whispered secrets untold but very wonderful, could one but understand.

On such a day the unreal became real, the impossible the possible by the magic of wind and cloud.

He though of the young Endymion, the wandering shepherd on Mount Ida's solitude, who on just such another day, in just such a leafy bower as the breaks ahead, waited the coming of his goddess.

Slade's gaze strayed toward the girl who rode by his side. Verily, she herself might be the sweet goddess, come down to earth to woo the sons of men.

Nonsense! said stern logic. But, there are more things —

So much for dreams and a vivid imagination! He laughed and turned his thoughts to mundane matters. The breaks might not hold goddesses, but they might well hold something less desirable. He gave his attention to his immediate surroundings.

The long train rolled slowly through the first line of breaks, the carters somewhat subdued because of the threatening weather. Their thoughts doubtless dwelt on the joys of Hardrock Hogan's Branding Pen Saloon.

Now the wind was rising fast, the sky growing darker and darker. Great shadows swept across the rangeland, the bending and straightening of the tall grasses.

Slade, the sheriff, and Estevan rode ahead, watchful and alert. On such a day anything could happen.

They were not very far from the second line of breaks when the storm broke in fury, with a wind of almost hurricane force howling from the southwest. The rain was a drenching downpour. Lightning flamed,

110

blue fire running along the grassheads. Deafening thunder crashed.

The cart horses squealed their fright, balked, tried to turn. But the drivers brought them under control, forced them on toward the dubious sanctuary of the breaks growth.

Shadow was not affected. Nor was Estevan's experienced mustang. The sheriff's mount was rather morose, but evidently somewhat calmed by association with the other not unduly disturbed cayuses following close behind Shadow.

The tempest grew even wilder. Wind, rain, lightning and thunder. But Slade maintained that it was the storm that saved them from probable disaster.

For as they dashed into the outer straggle of the breaks, his keen ears heard the squealing of the equally terrified outlaw horses.

Focusing his remarkable eyes straight ahead, he saw the five dancing shapes.

"Let them have it!" he roared, knowing that the posse was outlined against the brighter light of the outside prairie and that outlaw hands were streaking to holsters. He drew and shot with both hands, the others' guns booming almost in unison with the bellow of his Colts.

Two saddles were emptied. And the blazing gun battle was in full sway.

He heard a curse behind him, and another. His companions were both hit, but from the sound of their voices, not seriously. He continued to fire into the shadowy gloom as fast as he could squeeze trigger.

111

Another outlaw fell. Three down and two to go!

But the two still in their hulls, one tall and broad, spun their horses around and with raking spurs and lashing quirts sent them screaming into the teeth of the storm.

Slade had been so busy he had failed to note that the storm was abating. The wind was dropping fast, the rain had ceased falling, the thunder was muttering away into the east.

"Do you think one of the pair who got away was Messa?" the sheriff asked as Slade smeared a little antiseptic ointment on his grained ribs, following up with a patch for Estevan's cheek.

"I couldn't say for sure, never getting anything like a good look at him, but I'm inclined to think so," the Ranger replied. "His reaction and the way he took advantage of the opportunity was typically Messa.

"Well, anyhow, we didn't do bad. Got three of the devils."

"Yep, some more nice floor decorations," agreed the sheriff. "All right, boys," he told the carters, "Load 'em in with the others and let's get going."

Mary joined them, duly thankful that nobody was seriously injured.

"This day's work will mean another bonus," she told the carters who whooped their delight.

Even as the train left the breaks, the sun burst through the thinning clouds, funneling down a flood of golden light. Soon the sky was clean, rain-washed blue. Slickers were doffed and the hot sunshine quickly dried wet spots.

Slade was watchful during the last two breaks, although it seemed utterly to be beyond the realm of reason to think another attempt against the train might take place. But with such a character as Lance Messa he was taking no chances. Messa had proven himself a master of the unexpected.

However, nothing further untoward happened and at sunset the carts rolled into Sanderson, to learn that there had been quite a bit of flooding.

"And some time," Slade said with words of prophecy, gazing at the end wall of the long canyon, "there will be a real cloudburst striking a little to the north and they'll have a flood that will wash a good portion of this pueblo off the map."

The carts were lined up for loading, the horses cared for, and the carters boomed into Hardrock Hogan's Branding Pen Saloon to corral badly needed food and drink.

Mary had retired to her room in the Reagan House to change, clean up a little and rest briefly. So Slade and the sheriff took it easy at their table fortified with snorts and coffee, waiting to eat with her.

Didn't take her long to make herself presentable, as she phrased it, and soon they partook of the cook's best offerings.

The bodies had been carried to the sheriff's office where Deputy Blount received them and placed them on the floor for future inspection.

After they had finished eating and pipe and cigarette were going strong, Slade and the sheriff discussed the very nearly successful attempt to tie onto the cart train money. They agreed that where the trail entered the breaks was the least logical point for a try. In the past, any try had been made close to where the trail left the west fringe of the breaks, where escape routes were handy.

Yes, Messa had resorted to the unexpected.

"And if you hadn't been along, the chances are he would have made a go of it, storm or no storm," said the sheriff. "He still hasn't learned what has to be learned about *El Halcón*, though, and he never will. Time's running out fast for that horned toad."

Slade hoped he was right, and resolved to do his very best to prove him right.

"Well," Crane said, knocking out his pipe, "guess we'd better amble over to the office and give those carcasses a once-over and let folks come in for a look. Saxon and Hardrock will keep Mary company till we get back."

"And please don't go gallivanting off and getting mixed up in something," the girl begged. "I'd like to have a peaceful and pleasant evening."

They promised to do their best not to, and departed.

As they walked to the office, Crane glanced up at the cliffs, that were still oozing water.

"Yep, you're right," he said. "Some day this burg is going to get washed plumb into the Rio Grande."

Without misadventure, they reached the office to find quite a few people standing around, waiting to gain entrance.

"Take it easy," the sheriff told them. "We'll let you in shortly to look things over, if you want to. Just let us get our work done first."

114

CHAPTER
SEVENTEEN

Blount unlocked the door and they entered, the door being locked behind them, and began their examination of the bodies. The false beards were stripped off, revealing vicious looking countenances. "Worst looking bunch we've gotten hold of yet, especially the last three," said Crane.

Slade was inclined to agree with him. Former cowhands who haven't worked at it for a long time, was his diagnosis.

"Rather more money than the last bunch," the sheriff said as they emptied the pockets. "Well, there'll be less next time, on that I'll bet a hatful of pesos. The hellions would have been sittin' pretty if they'd managed to hang onto Hoskins *dinero*, and Saxon's poke today. But they didn't, so all's well. What did you say were the brands on those three horses the boys caught and brought in today?"

"Slickironed Arizona burns, I'd say," Slade replied. "Critters a long way from home. But that means nothing. Horses can be bought, traded, stolen, and end up a long way from where they were foaled."

"Yep, that's so," agreed Crane. "Well, shall we let folks in for a look at the carcasses?"

"Might as well," Slade answered. "Somebody might recall seeing them before."

However, it appeared nobody had, or if they had, they were not admitting it. The concensus of opinion was that they were mean looking specimens and had gotten just what they deserved.

"Figure Messa is drawing recruits from Arizona?" Slade asked after he had cleared the office.

"Logical to think so," Slade answered. "If we traced back on him, I wouldn't be surprised if we learned he had been mixed up in things over there and has a good reputation with owlhoots there, as a head man of a bunch. Doesn't matter to us. The fact is he is here and must be dealt with here."

"You'll 'dealt' him, no doubt in my mind as to that," was the cheerful rejoinder. "Okay, Blount, lock up and let's amble over to the Branding Pen before Mary begins getting the jitters, and I get a scolding. I'm scairt she thinks I'm bad company for Walt, always leading him into trouble."

"That I doubt," replied Blount. "I figure she knows nobody leads Walt. He does the leading. Let's go!"

The lights out and the door locked and they were on their way to the Branding Pen.

Without difficulty they reached the big saloon where the carters were already raising merry blue heck. They roared welcome and wanted to buy drinks.

"Will wonders never cease!" exclaimed Mary. "You did make it back without getting mixed up in something! Or did you? Never mind telling me, I want to dance."

116

Slade led her to the floor and they went through several numbers, the carters clapping and stamping applause.

They came back to the table for wine, coffee, and cigarettes, Mary rosy and breathless, her eyes sparkling, for the last number had been a fast one.

Estevan strolled in, bowed to *El Halcón* and glided to the kitchen, evidently with nothing of interest to report. For which Slade was not displeased. He felt he'd had enough activity for one day.

Mary felt the same way about it and gave Saxon the nod. He and his charges roared out, Slade, Mary and the sheriff following. The latter heading for his *casa*, and Slade and Mary for the Reagan House.

Late the following morning, while waiting for Doc Cooper to hold his inquest on the collection of bodies, Slade and the sheriff sat discussing the situation and wondering. Wondering what would be the elusive Lance Messa's next move. He had suffered a couple of setbacks, but Slade was convinced they would not slow him down. He'd be active without delay. And, same irritating old word, it was up to him and the sheriff to try and anticipate what his move would do. Which past experience had proven something of a chore, to put it mildly.

Fortunately, nobody had been killed in the course of the last two ruckuses, but Slade was fearful that the luck would not hold, with some innocent person being murdered. Which he earnestly hoped to prevent.

Soon Cooper arrived with his coroner's jury and held a brief inquest, the jury's verdict being that the

117

deceased met their deaths at the hands of law enforcement officers performing their duty and doing a good chore. Plant 'em and forget 'em, and bring in some more of the same brand! The undertaker took over. The sheriff regarded the bare floor with a disapproving eye, but taking comfort from his belief that it wouldn't be that way for long.

With the inquest out of the way and the sheriff busy with some paper work, Slade visited the cart station to find the loading going forward at a fast pace, the carters showing their appreciation of the latest bonus handed them.

"We'll finish today and be all set to roll for Echo tomorrow." Mary said. "I'm trying my darndest to keep up with the demand. Every cart I own is pressed into service for the Echo run, and I could use some more. Okay, be seeing you later; got to get back to work."

Leaving the carts, Slade walked slowly to the mouth of the canyon and stood gazing at the entrancing panorama of mountains and deserts that was the wastelands. He hoped they might provide him with inspiration, as they had done before.

But for the time at least, the towering peaks and crags stood immutable, guarding their secrets well, glowing in the sunshine, their cliffs reflecting like mirrors.

For a while longer he stood gazing, his eyes brooding, seeming to look into the far distances, the eyes of *El Halcón* on the trail that flowed over the next hilltop and into the beyond, with its never failing lure. With a sigh he turned and strolled uptown.

He was not far past the cart station when there sounded the boom of a shot, and a wild yelling. Facing away from the north, he turned to stare the way he had come. Another shot, more yelling. Slade started to speed in that direction, when around the corner of a near alley bulged four riders, quirting their horses.

"Look out!" a voice shouted. Hands gripping the butts of his Colts, Slade hurled himself down. Guns blazed, bullets screeched over him. He drew and shot with both hands as the riders swept past, saw one lurch wildly but stay in his hull. The arm of a second flew up, flapped down. Then the four were around a near corner and out of sight. Slade leaped to his feet, muttering wrathfully.

Now he located the source of the uproar, a saloon less than a block distant, from which men were boiling, some waving guns. Slade's voice thundered through the tumult,

"Hold it! Everything under control! What's going on here?"

"They shot Bayliss, the owner, grabbed the money," came a dozen answers.

"Hold it!" Slade repeated. "Please somebody fetch Sheriff Crane and somebody find Doc Cooper."

"It's Mr. Slade!" somebody shouted. "Right away, Mr. Slade, right away!"

Slade reached the saloon which was not very large but well furnished. He entered, hurried to the back room. He saw a broken chair, an overturned table. Lying on the floor, groaning and gulping, was a gray-haired man with blood streaming from his upper left shoulder.

Slade knelt beside him, swiftly examined the wound. No broken bones he could ascertain, but the bleeding must be stopped. He found the right spot, applied pressure. The bleeding lessened, very nearly stopped.

Estevan came racing in, gripping the haft of his knife, looking as if he would use it on anybody who got in his way. Nobody did.

"To the Branding Pen and get what I'll need," Slade told him. "Hurry!"

Estevan sped out. Slade shifted his strained position, and continued to apply pressure.

A hand slipped over his and gently replaced it. A very small hand but capable.

"Good girl!" Slade said. "Always right where you're needed most."

"I hope so," she said softly.

Estevan returned in a surprisingly short time with all that was needful.

Very quickly Slade had the wound smeared with ointment, padded, taped and bandaged. He rocked back on his heels and surveyed his handiwork, then nodded with satisfaction. The bandage was barely stained.

Bayliss had stopped groaning and gulping and was looking up wonderingly at his benefactor.

"Feel better?" Slade asked.

"A lot," the saloon owner replied, his voice a trifle shaky.

120

"I think you'll be more comfortable in a chair," Slade told him. "Keep perfectly still, now, relax. Don't move your arm."

Bayliss was a big man, but Slade picked him up easily and placed him in the chair Mary had shoved forward. Slade rolled a cigarette for him which he received gratefully, and lighted it.

Bayliss puffed hard.

"And now suppose you tell me just what happened, as well as you can," Slade suggested.

"I was reaching for my money poke that I was going to pack to the bank when I heard a sound. Standing behind me were those four bewhiskered devils. Guess they came in by way of that back door that was supposed to be locked, but I reckon wasn't. One made a grab for the poke. I tried to pull it back but another one, a big tall one, shot me. Then they shot a few holes in the ceiling and hightailed."

"I see," Slade said. "Rather new to this section, Mr. Bayliss?"

"Yes, I guess I am," the owner admitted. "I came from over east."

"Well, let this be a lesson to you not to have large sums of money lying around to tempt gents with share-the-wealth notions," Slade advised. "The next time might even be more serious. Take my advice."

"I will," Bayliss promised devoutly.

The sheriff came rumbling in. "Was out and they had to look me up," he explained his delay. "What the blazes happened?"

Bayliss's story was relayed. He swore, under his mustache in deference to Mary's presence.

"No carcasses?" he asked of Slade.

"A couple nicked, not sure how badly," the Ranger replied.

"You're slippin'," Crane declared. "Should have gotten all four."

"I was lucky I was not the one 'got'," Slade answered. "Was very sudden and most unexpected."

Doc Cooper strolled in. "Was told Walt had taken charge, so didn't feel there was any need to hurry," he said. He glanced at Slade's treatment of the wound, nodded approval.

"Put him to bed and make him take it easy," he ordered. "He'll be okay. Walt never makes a mistake where such matters are concerned. Give him all the hot coffee he will drink. That's good for shock and loss of blood. I'll look in on him later."

"And I'm going back to work," Mary said. "Saxon may be in need of me."

"Okay, I'll see you later," Slade promised. "And thanks again for your help. You're mighty handy to have around."

Mary smiled a trifle wistfully, and trotted out. Slade and the sheriff returned to the office to relieve Deputy Blount.

"Figure it was Messa and his bunch?" the sheriff asked of Slade.

"I couldn't say for sure," *El Halcón* replied. "I never got a good look at the four when they went past me. I was too busy trying to keep my hide from being

122

punctured to search out individuals. Bayliss said the one who shot him was big, but that was rather vague and could apply to any number of people. It was like one of Messa's capers, but that's as far as I'm ready to go. Although I wouldn't be too surprised if they were some of his bunch even if he didn't happen to be along."

"Anyhow if it was Messa or some of his bunch they made a good haul, from what Bayliss told me, and are well heeled again, for a while," Crane remarked. "Bayliss said he didn't mind the loss of the money so much, he's insured, but he'd sure like a chance to even the score with the devil who shot him. I told him he might get the chance. Was thinking maybe he might be like Vandyke, the former Wallop owner, and his bartender with their double-barreled shotguns that blew a couple of owlhoots to Hades." Slade smiled and didn't argue the point.

They had some coffee from the back room and a couple of smokes, then chatted together for a while, discussing Messa and his antics.

Finally Slade pinched out his cigarette and glanced at the darkening window panes.

"Guess we might as well amble to the Branding Pen," he suggested. "Mary should be through with her loading chore by now."

"Yep, might as well lock up and mosey," the sheriff agreed. "Be sure dark by the time we get there, and I crave a snort, or a couple of them. All set, gents?"

Walking slowing, pausing to glance in windows now and then, they reached the Branding Pen without difficulty on the way. Where the carters, their day's work finished, were already whooping it up.

Mary had not put in an appearance yet, so they sat down to await her arrival before ordering dinner.

Estevan peered in from the kitchen, bowed to *El Halcón*, and shook his head. Slade smiled and waved to him.

The Bayliss saloon robbery was a prime topic of conversation. Hardrock and others came over to discuss the matter with Slade and the sheriff.

Slade repeated Bayliss' story, the sheriff adding some pungent comments. The carters were spreading their own version of the affair. Which, though perhaps straying from the facts a mite, was the most interesting, and highly complimentary to Slade.

Mary arrived, gay, vivacious, and hungry! The orders were sent to the kitchen at once.

They ate their dinner with the appetite of perfect digestion, and enjoyed it greatly. Then snorts, wine, coffee, pipe, and cigarettes.

"The loading and unloading are nice, but I really believe I like the open road best," Mary remarked. "With the sun and the wind, and the prairie grasses swaying and bending. And then the derricks reaching up to the blue of the sky. I'm plumb anxious to be rolling."

"Just a wildcatter at heart," chuckled the sheriff. "What do you think, Walt?"

"I'm inclined to think you are right," Slade replied smilingly. "Most any day now and she'll be buying a drilling rig and setting out for a new field."

"If you'll find me a field, and I'll take all my carters along," Mary giggled.

"And that would sure liven up the oil business," the sheriff declared with conviction.

"I sometimes think it could stand a little livening up," Mary said. "Acquiring a lot of money is inclined to make folks stodgy."

"Guess you should know," commented the sheriff.

"I refuse to be catalogued as stodgy," the girl retorted. "Do you think I'm stodgy, Walt?"

"Not noticeably so," the Ranger replied.

"And this argument is getting exactly nowhere," said Crane. "Let us drink!"

So the hours passed with laughter and jest. But there was a long and hard day in the offing and they called it an early night.

CHAPTER
EIGHTEEN

The following morning justified Mary's contention that rolling the carts was the best part of the business. A morning of blue and gold and amethyst, with birds singing, and a fragrant breeze blowing.

Even the usually stolid cart horses were affected and snorted gaily and tossed their heads.

As a matter of habit, Slade and Estevan scouted ahead, alert and watchful, although Slade could not conceive an attack on the loaded train. Just best to take no chances with such an individual as Lance Messa.

They passed through the welcome shade of the first line of breaks, with only the birds to comment on their passing. The second was a repeat of the first. As was the third. Then the fourth, and the smoke smudge of Echo staining the sky.

"Looks good," Mary said. "Another successful run. And no trouble on the way, which also helps."

The carts rolled to the station. They were placed in line for unloading, the horses cared for.

Lerner was present with his tally sheets. Also, a number of owners and their hands. A snack and a drink, and then the unloading began, with still several hours of daylight.

"Which is better than flares," Lerner said. "Less grease and smoke."

Estevan glided into the Diehard kitchen. The sheriff wished to have a gab with Rader, the Diehard owner.

"Suppose you'll amble up to Lerner's place?" he asked Slade.

"Yes, I suppose so," Slade replied.

"Okay, but watch your step," Crane admonished. Slade promised to do so.

Swinging into the saddle, he rode slowly across the bowl, but not straight to the oil magnate's quarters, for he was restless and had no desire to be cooped up till dark. Which also applied to Shadow, who never liked being cooped up.

"Just got a notion it would be a good idea to amble up the cut," he told the horse. "A hunch? Really, I don't know but could be. This is the way the darn things start. So let's go!"

Shadow snorted decided agreement and they entered the cut. They passed a number of workers, who shouted greetings. Slade replied to the greeting, but did not draw rein.

Nor at the building machine shop, nor the yards. He knew the surveyors, with their transit, measuring rod and stick pins and stakes, were some distance out on the prairie, staking out the right-of-way, which the steel would follow.

He rode on slowly, his gaze sweeping the rangeland in every direction. He knew the survey was still on Van Rice's Bar M holding and would be for some time. He determined to have a talk with Rice soon and try to learn just how he stood in relation to the railroad. Slade had a feeling that, present conditions continuing to prevail, he and Rice might hit it off together.

Finally, rounding a stand of thicket, he saw the surveyors. To their right was a long, brush-covered hill, not a very high hill, that was the beginning of a shallow clutter of breaks. They were evidently getting ready to knock off work for the day. For they were collecting their tools and packing them into their horse drawn cart.

Slade rode on and was some six hundred yards from his quarry when loud and clear sounded the clang of a rifle, the report coming from the brush-covered hill.

The slug must have come close, for the surveyors ducked wildly and rushed to the dubious cover of the cart.

Another shot, more ducking. Looked like the hidden rifleman really meant business. Foolish to gamble that he didn't. Slade decided the little game had gone far enough.

Whipping out his heavy, long-range Winchester, a special made to order for him by Jaggers Dunn, he lined sights with the hill crest, squeezed the trigger.

The big rifle rang out like thunder. Slade fired again and again, holding the first shot a bit, dropping the next one and those that followed into the brush that crested the hill.

Another moment and sapling tops waved wildly. As to whether he had nicked or killed some hellion, he didn't know, or care, but there was no doubt that somebody was going away from there, fast. And no more shots sounded from the hill.

Reloading, Slade rode on to where the surveyors were shouting and swearing, and shaking their fists at the hilltop. They recognized *El Halcón* and bawled a greeting.

Reaching them, Slade drew rein. The transit man in charge of the crew reached up to shake hands.

"You sure came along at a good time, Mr. Slade," he said. "Those bullets were coming uncomfortably close. Figured in another minute he might get the range."

"First time anything like this has happened?" Slade asked.

"Yes, the first time out here on the prairie," came the reply. "You'll remember somebody fired a shot into the breakthrough the day before the celebration — you were there but this is the first time since then."

"Okay," Slade said. "Tomorrow I'll have a couple of men with rifles accompanying you. If some hellion hankers to play games, we'll try and accommodate. All set to go? Let's be heading for town. Will be dark before so very long."

They got under way, the surveyors chattering and speculating, casting admiring glances at *El Halcón* from time to time.

Slade was mostly silent, for he was pondering just what the meaning of the episode was, and just what might be behind it. The drygulcher might have just been firing warning shots, but there was no guarantee that was so. The business certainly demanded explanation. He resolved to get in touch with Van Rice, the Bar M owner, as quickly as possible.

They reached town before full dark, with the surveyors shouting their goodbyes as Slade turned off toward Lerner's quarters.

After taking care of Shadow, who seemed bored with the whole affair, Slade repaired to the quarters where he found Crane awaiting him.

"Well how goes it? was his greeting.

Slade told him, in detail, just what happened. The sheriff indulged in some fancy swearing.

"Figure Rice was back of it?" he concluded.

"Frankly I don't know," Slade admitted. "He never struck me as a person who would go in for such a thing, but I could be mistaken about him. Also, as we both know, a owner's riders will sometimes get out of hand and commit acts he wouldn't countenance. That angle must also be given thought. No, I don't know for sure about Van Rice, but I certainly intend to find out." He was silent for a few minutes, then —

"Somehow I have a feeling — call it a hunch, if you will — that our *amigo* Lance Messa is mixed up in the deal. As to that, I also don't know for sure, but I'll assure you I intend to give it some very serious thought."

"Expect you're plumb right where that sidewinder is concerned," the sheriff growled. "Well, it's full dark. Suppose we mosey down to the Diehard for a few snorts and a bite or two of chuck. Mary has already come and gone. I've a notion she's sorta put out with you for gallivanting off without telling her what you intended to do, but I reckon you'll be able to bear up under the strain. Okay? Let's go!"

Without untoward incident of any kind, they reached the Diehard, to find Mary at their table awaiting them, with Lerner and Deputy Arbaugh keeping her company.

"No use scolding him," she told the sheriff. "Just as senseless as pouring water on a duck's back hoping to wet the duck. He *will* go gallivanting. But he always comes back, and that's what really counts. Now that he is here, let's eat while we've got the chance." Her hearers agreed heartily. "And a couple of snorts to lay a foundation," said the sheriff. "Waiter!"

After a good dinner, everybody felt better. Slade toyed with a cup of coffee, Mary with a glass of wine. The sheriff did not toy with his snorts, but put them away pronto.

"Will finish the unloading tomorrow without difficulty," Lerner said, riffling his check sheets.

"Yes, could have time for a bit of a rest before rolling the empties," Mary said. "Chances are I'll hold over until two days after tomorrow. The boys need a little relaxation.

"And so do the horses," she added. "They too have been doing a prime chore. Another day of rest with extra helpings of oats are their bonus."

"And must never be forgotten or taken as a matter of course," Slade said. "We'd be lost without them."

"Yes," the sheriff said soberly. "Never neglect the little critters the Good Lord gives under your hand."

All evening, Slade kept a close watch for Van Rice, but the Bar M owner did not put in an appearance.

As it began to get quite late, Slade said a few words to Estevan and the knife man made the rounds of the other bars, with negative results. Looked like Rice was not coming to town. Not tonight, anyway.

Slade resolved on a personal contact with Rice, but did not mention his decision.

Although exhilarated by the prospect of the holiday, everybody was very tired and did not stay up overly late.

CHAPTER
NINETEEN

While the last of the unloading was under way the following morning, Slade rode through the breakthrough and turned more to the west, following the line of the right-of-way.

He reached the point where the surveyors were busy at their chore, the two riflemen lounging about and keeping a watchful eye on everything. The crew greeted him with enthusiasm.

"Any further trouble," he asked the transit man, who shook his head.

"Nothing out of the way has happened, and I figure nothing will with you on the job, Mr. Slade," he replied.

"Hope you're right," Slade smiled and kept on riding, veering a little to the north.

He had covered some three miles, when from behind a stand of thicket a little to the north of where he rode came a crackle of shots and a drumming of hoofs. He reined in, dropping a hand to the butt of his Winchester.

Around the growth came a single rider, bending low in the saddle, spurring his mount. He was bearing down on Slade and but a short distance away when his horse stepped into a marmot hole and went sprawling, flinging his rider to the ground, hard.

And as he went down, Slade recognized the rider as Van Rice, the Bar M owner.

Around the brush bulged four more riders, shooting at the prostrate Rice, who was partly shielded by his horse, which had also regained its feet, one fore foot hanging. No doubt but murder was in the making. There was not a moment to lose.

Whipping his Winchester from the saddle boot, Slade let drive.

One of the killers spun from his saddle to lie motionless. Slade fired again and saw a second drygulcher lurch in the saddle, grab the horn for support.

But all three jerked their horses about and streaked around the growth, Slade speeding them on their way with lead. He listened a moment to the dimming hoofbeats, then with a swift glance at the dead outlaw, who was incapable of further harm, turned his attention to Rice, who had also regained his feet looking dazed.

"My God, Mr. Slade, did you show at just the right time!" he gasped. "I figured I was a goner for sure."

"Hurt?" Slade asked.

"Just shook up," the rancher replied.

"Know who tried to drygulch you?"

"Why — why," Rice hesitated, "some of the railroaders, I guess. They don't seem to have much use for us, but why they would try to kill me, I don't know. I —"

"Take a look at that dead devil's hands and tell me what you learn."

134

Rice did as he was told, looked up with a bewildered expression, just as Slade expected.

"Railroaders don't have the scars of rope and branding irons on their hands," he said impressively.

"Yesterday a bunch posing as cowhands shot up the surveying crew," he added. Rice looked even more bewildered.

"Mr. Slade, won't you please tell me what it means?" he begged. "I'm completely flabbergasted. I wouldn't think of making trouble for Mr. Dunn and his railroad. I admire him too much, just as I admire you, Mr. Slade."

"Outside interference," Slade replied briefly. "I happen to know your ranch house is nearby."

"Yes, I was making for it when those hellions started throwing lead at me," Rice interpolated.

"So let's go there, where we can talk without interruption," Slade suggested. "Wait till I look things over here. You're sure you are all right?"

"I'm fine," Rice replied.

The injury to his horse proved slight, just a sprain. The outlaw cayuse, a well trained and intelligent-appearing beast, had remained beside its fallen master.

"You can ride it and lead your critter," Slade said. To the dead outlaw he gave but a casual glance, jerking free its false beard and dropping it in his saddle pouch.

"The sheriff will give it an examination." he explained. "All set? Let's go."

"I've a notion it was lucky for me that my horse did take a header," Rice remarked as they mounted. "Sorta threw those scoundrels off balance and gave you time to get into action."

Slade nodded agreement, and swept the prairie with an all embracing glance that made sure there were no more drygulchers in the vicinity.

Very shortly they reached the Bar M ranch house, which Slade had visited before. Rice called a wrangler who was formally introduced to Shadow and led the big black and the other horses to the barn and mangers of oats.

"And please send somebody to Echo to fetch Sheriff Crane," Slade requested. "Should find him at Lerner's place or at the Diehard Saloon."

"Right away," Rice replied and gave the wrangler instructions.

They entered the ranch house which boasted a comfortable and well furnished sitting room.

"And now a drink, or coffee?"

"Coffee, please," Slade said.

Rice called his old cook whom Slade had met on a former occasion, and gave the order, his own being a drink.

"Sorta' feel the need of one after my shaking up," he chuckled.

Slade shook hands with the cook who hurried to his kitchen to return shortly with his employer's drink and Slade's steaming coffee.

For a while they sipped and smoked in silence, which Rice finally broke.

"I believe you said something about outside interference, Mr. Slade," he remarked suggestively.

136

"Yes, I did," Slade conceded. "Outside interference on the part of somebody playing for big stakes, a million dollars, or so. Or so he thinks, and anxious to cause trouble to the railroad and the ranchers to further his scheme."

Rice looked more bewildered than ever. "I'll have to admit I just don't understand," he said.

For another moment, Slade smoked in silence. Abruptly he arrived at a decision.

In terse sentences, he told the astounded rancher about Lance Messa and his scheme to acquire rights to the great oil pool, most of which was under Bar M land.

Rice listened, shaking his head in astonishment and not speaking until Slade paused in his discourse.

"Why, Mr. Slade," he said, "I've no objection to somebody managing to tap that oil pool you say is under my land. Let them go ahead and drill. They are welcome to anything they can tie onto, just so they don't bother me with it. I'm not interested in a lot of money, Mr. Slade. I'm a cattleman, and my cows provide me with a comfortable living and that should be as much as an old bachelor on the wrong side of forty should ask."

He paused a moment, regarding *El Halcón*, chuckled a little, shaking his head again.

"And Mr. Slade," he said, "I've a notion you feel about the same way."

"I do," Slade admitted.

"One thing about you sorta' puzzles me," Rice continued. "I can't quite understand how a man of your undoubted outstanding ability is content to be just a deputy sheriff."

Slade smiled. Seeing as he had taken Rice into his confidence so far, he figured he might as well go whole hog.

From a cunningly concealed pocket in his broad leather belt he took something that caught the light, and laid it on the table between them. Rice stared at the object, his eyes widening.

It was a gleaming silver star set on a silver circle, the feared and honored badge of the Texas Rangers!

"So that's what you are," Rice said slowly. "Well, I might have known it. I might have known it! You do things as only a Ranger can do them. If this don't take the hide off the barn door! *El Halcón*, a Texas Ranger!"

"Yes, I'm a Ranger," Slade said. "Undercover man for Captain McNelty.

"Please forget you saw this, Mr. Rice," he said as he restored the badge to its hiding place. "I'd like to stay undercover in this section for a while yet, if possible."

"Never even saw it," Rice chuckled. "My eyes are mighty bad at times, conveniently so!"

They laughed together and drank some coffee, the cook hurrying in to replenish Slade's cup and plump another drink in front of the ranch owner.

For some time they sat talking, smoking, comfortably relaxed. Slade raised his head at the beat of fast hoofs approaching.

"Should be Tom," he remarked.

The beats ceased and the sheriff came hurrying in, his face mirroring concern. He drew a breath of relief and addressed Slade.

138

"Wrangler who brought the word said you and Rice were settin' in the house talking, but I had to make sure. Well, got any carcasses for me? He winked at Rice, who grinned.

"Down the trail about a quarter of a mile you'll find one," Slade replied. "Guess you took the short cut here and didn't see it."

The sheriff sighed resignedly and turned his attention to Van Rice.

"You follow a drunk by the bottles along the way, but you follow Slade by the carcasses," he said. "All right, lead me to it. First tell me how you managed to collect it."

He listened attentively to Slade's description, which was ably supplemented by Rice, sipping the drink the cook set before him.

"I don't think you'll be bothered any more by drygulchers shooting from hilltops," Rice observed. "My boys will take care of that. And I intend to have a talk with owners to the north and west to make sure they don't get any wrong notions about the railroad."

"Thanks," Slade replied. "That will help."

"Glad to do anything I can to help," Rice said. "Another drink for the sheriff, Butch."

The cook hustled in with one and insisted on Slade having more coffee.

CHAPTER
TWENTY

"Well," said the sheriff when he shoved back his empty glass, "I reckon we'd better pick up that carcass and pack it to town."

"I'll have the wrangler hitch up my little wagon and take care of that chore," Rice offered.

"That'll be good," Slade accepted. "And give him the outlaw horse for his trouble. It's a good looking cayuse."

Rice promised to do so.

"I'll be in the Diehard tonight, the chances are," he called after the wagon was hitched up and they got under way. "See you there."

The slain outlaw was pronounced an ornery specimen by Crane and the wrangler. Slade thought him about average of his brand. He had once been a cowhand, Slade believed, although the scars on his hands were so old as to be hardly discernible.

When they reached the point where the surveyors were at work, they faced a barrage of questions which they answered as Slade saw they should be. A cheer was raised when the crew was assured that, due to the kindness of Rice, they need have no fear of further drygulching.

140

A pause where the workers on the yards and machine shop were assembled was also thought advisable. They, too, were greatly pleased at the news of Rice's cooperation.

The passage of the wagon with its grisly burden through the streets to Lerner's stable kicked up considerable excitement and resulted in questions the sheriff answered as he saw fit. The keeper soon cleared his stable of the curious, however.

Shadow and the sheriff's horse were cared for and Slade and Crane headed for the cart station and the Diehard. It was now well past the middle of the afternoon.

"And you took Rice in tow," the sheriff remarked. "I don't know how you do it! I don't know how you do it!"

"Taking him in tow, as you express it, wasn't difficult," Slade replied. "I merely put the truth in front of him and he was at once in accord.

"That's the way with most people. More trouble is the result of misunderstandings than of cussedness," he added.

"But the cussedness attracts the most attention," Crane chuckled.

Which Slade had to admit was so.

Reaching the cart station, they found the unloading just about finished, the carters getting ready to start their holiday with their bonus money in their pockets. Soon business in the Diehard, and other places, would pick up.

Mary was also making ready to call it a day. First, however, before heading to her room, she demanded an explanation of their misdoings.

The sheriff obliged, in his own inimitable fashion. Mary was able to read between the lines, and reserved scoldings until later.

After a final glance around to make sure everything was as it should be, she kissed Slade lightly and scampered off, smiling indulgently as they watched her go.

Slade and the sheriff retired to the Diehard to give her time to change and rest a bit before ordering their dinner. The sheriff was looking reflective.

"I was just wondering," he said, "why did those devils try to kill Rice?"

"Perhaps Messa, with his usual acumen, decided that he would be a hard man to handle and that a new owner might be easier," Slade answered. "Just guess work on my part, of course, but it could be the explanation."

"Think they might try it again?"

"I doubt it," Slade decided. "They know he'll be very much on the alert from now on, and so will be his riders. I feel they will conclude that what might be gained isn't worth the risk involved. However, I am going to tell Estevan to have one of his knife men keep an eye on Rice when he's in town. That should keep him safe."

"You're darn right," the sheriff growled. "I hope Messa makes a personal try at doing Rice in with the knife man tailing him. Then we wouldn't be bothered with Messa any more."

"Too much to hope for, I fear," Slade smiled.

The sheriff glanced around and muttered under his mustache, shaking his head.

"This place is going to be a madhouse before the night is over," he grumbled.

Slade thought he was very likely right, but only laughed. For he was forced to admit to himself that he rather liked madhouses, especially because there was always the chance that the antics of the denizens of one might result in opportunity.

And at the moment he felt he needed opportunity badly. He hadn't the slightest idea what Messa was up to, or where he might strike and when.

That he would strike, and soon, Slade was convinced. But there leering at him were the old irritating questions, Where? and When?

Oh, well, he hadn't been doing so bad of late, and maybe the luck would continue to hold. He dismissed the whole business from his mind for the time being and relaxed with his coffee and cigarette.

He had learned from past experience that dwelling too long and too assiduously on a problem was liable to retard rather than advance its solution. To heck with it! He'd join the carters in celebrating their holiday.

However, when Estevan opened the kitchen door a crack and shook his head, he did cross to the kitchen and gave him instructions relative to Van Rice.

"Will do," said the Yaqui-Mexican and drifted out the back door to relay the instructions to an *amigo*.

143

Slade returned to the sheriff confident that did Van Rice come to town, every move he made would be watched, and if advisable, guarded against.

The carters roared in and the sheriff's madhouse was soon well under way.

Was beginning to go strong when Mary danced in, her cheeks rosy, her eyes sparkling. She plumped into a chair close to Slade's and sipped the glass of wine a waiter placed before her.

"Of course I'm hungry," she replied to the sheriff's question. "Did you ever know me to be otherwise? Oh, my poor figure!"

The sheriff snorted derisively, let his gaze rove up and down, then twinkled his eyes at her. Mary took the implied compliment in stride and smiled at him.

Glances from various directions confirmed the sheriff's compliment. Which without doubt was duly noted by Miss Merril, although she refrained from mentioning the fact. She returned to her initial complaint, that she was hungry. As it happened, her companions, including Lerner who dropped in riffling his check sheets, also felt the need of nourishment. Which matter was called to the cook's attention.

He, without delay, set about remedying the situation.

And when the viands arrived, it was conceded by all that they were worth waiting for. Plates were cleaned to the last smidgen, the highest compliment that could be paid the master of the kitchen and his helpers.

So the holiday got off to an excellent start, with the carters really getting down to business, to which the quivering rafters and jumping lights bore witness.

"Yep, nothing like laying a good foundation of chuck if you expect the redeye to properly cooperate," said the sheriff sampling his glass and nodding approval.

Slade felt the same about his final cup of fragrant coffee and his cigarette, Mary about her glass of wine.

With his mind clearing up, Slade felt he had been wise to dismiss the whole Messa problem from his thoughts for the time being. Now he was developing a hunch that said something of importance would very likely come along to lend a hand. Which was all to the good. He would remain receptive and refrain from trying to force the issue. Let future developments take care of themselves. He would just relax and enjoy himself until inspiration saw fit to come.

The wisdom of the course would before so very long be verified.

Now the Diehard was truly swinging a wide loop. Railroaders, oil field workers, and others, evidently felt it was their duty to assist the carters in making their holiday one to remember, and were doing so to the very best of their ability.

Mary wanted to dance, so she and Slade had a "wrestling match," as the sheriff phrased it, on the crowded floor.

"Rough and rowdy, but I loved it," the girl declared breathlessly as they returned to the table after three numbers. "Wouldn't you like to give it a whirl, Uncle Tom?"

"I think too much of my rheumatics," the sheriff declined.

After a period of rest, Mary and Lerner decided to take another chance on the floor.

Deputy Arbaugh had dropped in and was discussing a drink when Estevan entered and came straight to the table, his eyes glittering.

"*Capitán*," he said, "the *Señor* Rice in the Wallop Saloon is. I think he intends to soon leave."

"Yes?" Slade answered. "Is he alone?"

"*Si, Capitán*, but at the corner of the alley that is the saloon behind stand four whiskered *hombres* who the swing doors watch, grumbling themselves among. Very closely they the doors watch. The *Señor* Rice they plan to harm, I fear."

"I think you're right," Slade said, rising to his feet. "All right, let's go. Only hope we're not too late."

He waved to Mary on the floor, and with the sheriff, the deputy, and Estevan crowding close behind him, headed north on the packed street, veering a block to the east.

"We'll enter the alley from the east and ease down it, fast, and be behind the devils," he explained.

Despite the crowds on the streets, they made good progress. But to Slade, fully aware of the rancher's danger, the distance seemed to stretch without end.

However, to the anxious Ranger's relief, they reached the alley without any alarm sounding and sped down it until they saw the four killers, staring at the swinging doors and muttering among themselves.

"Gents," Slade called softly, "you're looking in the wrong direction."

146

There was a chorus of startled exclamations, hands streaking to holsters, and the street rocked to the blaze of gunfire.

Weaving, ducking, Slade shot with both hands, the sheriff's and the deputy's guns boomed beside him.

Two of the drygulchers fell at that first thundering volley. Estevan's knife hissed and a third was down. The fourth devil lined sights with Slade's breast, but the Ranger hurled himself sideways, both Colts spurting fire, and there were four bodies on the ground. The whole bloody affair had taken little more than ten seconds.

A moment of utter silence in the saloon, and then the Wallop madhouse dwarfed the Diehard's best efforts of the evening. Men boiled through the swinging door, shouting, swearing, bellowing questions.

"Shut up!" bawled the sheriff. "Shut up, I say! This is the Law speaking."

The tumult died to a hum.

"Rice, where are you?" Slade called.

The rancher came hurrying to him looking gravely concerned.

"What's it all about, Mr. Slade?" he asked.

"You're going down to the Diehard as soon as we clean up this mess. Then we'll talk," Slade replied. "Take it easy, I don't think you have anything more to worry about, but this one tonight was serious." He turned to Estevan and said.

"Hustle down to the Diehard and fetch Lerner and some of the carters, including Saxon. You know about how many we'll need. Sure *La Señorita* may come along if she wishes to."

Estevan nodded and sped away.

The sheriff glanced at Slade before answering the questions with which he was being bombarded.

"Just a try at a drygulching that didn't work," Slade said. "We sort of got the jump on the hellions."

That seemed to satisfy the Wallop crowd. Apparently they presumed it was the sheriff and his posse the slain owlhoots tried to drygulch. Which was what Slade desired them to think, stilling the questioning. He and the sheriff stripped off the false beards and invited the crowd to take a look. They were pronounced ornery looking horned toads. The Wallop head bartender was certain they had been in the saloon earlier. Some of the Wallop patrons believed they too had noticed them, but were vague about it.

Slade had glanced at their hands and concluded they had once been range riders which he did not mention.

"Look them over a bit more when we get them to the stable," he told Crane who nodded his understanding.

Estevan arrived with Lerner, Saxon, and a number of hilarious carters, who appeared to welcome the chore as a frolicsome addition to the holiday.

Mary sent word that, learning everybody was all right, she was staying right where she was, with Rader. They could brief her on the incident when they returned to the Diehard.

"Guess she's seen enough carcasses of late to hold her for a while," was the sheriff's comment.

148

The bodies were packed to the stable, which was nearby, and laid out on the floor.

Slade and the sheriff agreed that further examination could wait until the next day. Then with their companions, including Van Rice, they headed for the Diehard, reaching the peaceful madhouse without further excitement on the way.

Mary and Rader were given a detailed account of the affair. Both congratulated Rice on his escape.

"And as I said, I feel very sure that you'll not be bothered again," Slade told the rancher.

"I keep getting deeper and deeper in your debt all the time, Mr Slade," Rice sighed.

"Lending a hand where it is needed by the deserving is a pleasure," the Ranger replied.

"You have plenty of company, Mr. Rice," Mary told him smilingly. "In every direction, he has folks in debt to him."

"That I can believe," the rancher replied.

The period of excitement had inspired the Diehard crowd to make even more noise. The holiday was rapidly approaching the status of an outstanding celebration.

Which, despite the racket and the smoke, Slade regarded complacently and with a feeling of satisfaction. He was well pleased with how things had worked out. Later he would be less pleased with the night. For other members of the outlaw bunch were far from idle.

CHAPTER
TWENTY-ONE

The railroad short line that tapped Tumble and Echo had its inception some miles to the south of Tumble, where it made connections with the great East-West line. From south of Tumble the steel ran mostly over level prairie, well ballasted and kept in excellent repair. For it did plenty of business, freight and passenger.

At the point of juncture there were two long sidings to accommodate the trains of tank cars filled with oil, and the returning empties. Well up on one siding stood a locomotive purring with a full head of steam, its fire banked. After the local that followed the westbound Flyer had paused to discharge or take on passengers, it would haul the short-line train to Tumble and Echo.

On the other siding, close to where it joined the East-West, was a single boxcar.

Nearby was a small shack where passengers waiting for trains sought shelter in bad weather, especially if the short-line train had not yet arrived from Tumble. Then its coaches would provide shelter for those who planned to catch the East-West local to Sanderson and points west.

In the shack was a telegraph instrument. But there was no operator at night.

The East-West westbound Flyer was just about due. Stack booming steam streaked black smoke, side rods clanking, steel tires grinding the rails, it roared through the night, its two long and two short whistle blasts signaled crossings, the mellow notes flinging back a hundred shattered echoes from the mountain cliffs.

There was a slow order past the junction, so the engineer eased his throttle a little, applied the brakes a trifle gently, peering ahead.

The junction passed and he widened the throttle, The Flyer thundered on, its headlight beam questing ahead. In its iron brain, perhaps — who knows — visions of sunny California and the blue Pacific.

And some distance behind, came the short local. Like the Dog Star's pup following the Dog Star across the sky.

The local made plenty of speed, but it paused at places the lordly Flyer would not admit existed.

Silence followed, broken only by the low-voiced conversation of the Tumble train crew waiting in their caboose for the local to arrive.

No, not quite the only sound. There was still another, a slight clicking as a manual car mover beat lightly against the boxcar's rear wheels.

The boxcar was moving, very slowly. Down the siding toward the East-West main line. It neared the switch and stopped, one corner hanging over the main line.

Four bearded men disengaged from its shadow and moved back a little farther from the main line.

In an attitude of waiting, they stood gazing eastward toward where the local's headlight beam would split the gloom.

It appeared, shimmering and glowing, as the engineer blew four signals.

Out of deference to the slow order, he almost closed his throttle, lightly applied the brakes. Peering ahead in quest of possible signals, he saw the headlight beam outline the corners of the boxcar hanging over the main line. Vainly he slammed the throttle shut, spun the brake handle.

With a rending crash, the locomotive hit the car, knocking it to splinters. The engine did not turn over but was derailed, as was the express car.

Followed a hideous pandemonium. The screams and cries of cut, bruised and frightened passengers, the wholehearted cursing of the engine crew, the bellow of steam from broken pipes, the crackling of flames from the splintered boxcar that, loaded with inflammable materials, had caught fire from scattered coals. Luckily, it had been knocked some little distance from the coaches.

The express messenger swung his side door open to peer out. He tried to close it but from the growth a gun blazed and he fell to the floor, screaming hoarsely, blood streaming from his upper right arm.

From the close-by scattering of growth bulged four bearded men, one tall and broad.

The big man leaped into the express car, while his companions fired along the line of coaches to keep the train crew and the passengers inside.

152

The messenger had been checking the contents of his safe for the Sanderson crew change and the door stood open.

The bit man bounded to it and began to transfer rolls of gold coin and thick packets of large bills into a sack he carried. Very quickly he finished the chore and leaped to the ground without a glance at the moaning messenger. He and his companions vanished from sight. Another instant and fast hoofs beat westward.

The shooting stopped, the conductor and a brakeman raced to the scene of the wreck. Were met by the cursing, burned and bruised engine crew, neither of whom was seriously injured.

It was different with the express messenger who was without doubt bleeding to death.

By great good fortune there was a doctor, with his satchel aboard the local. Summoned by the conductor's calls for help, he took over and quickly had the dangerous flow of blood stanched. Neither the engine crew or the passengers were seriously hurt, but he was a busy man for a while, just the same.

The Tumble train crew had arrived on the scene to help straighten things out.

"The only thing to do," said their conductor, "is load everybody into your coaches and take them to Tumble, where we can send a wire to Sanderson to send the wrecker and help."

The chore was quickly accomplished. The doctor would remain with the injured messenger until help arrived. The local's train crew would wait in the shack.

Flags had been sent out in both directions to halt oncoming traffic.

The short train raced to Tumble at top speed, arriving at the oil town without incident. Wires were sent in every direction, to Sanderson, Echo and elsewhere. One to Sheriff Crane who was said to be at Echo, which he was.

Otherwise, there was nothing anybody could do for the time being, except to care for the local passengers who were not destined for Tumble and Echo.

Sheriff Crane was in the Diehard with Slade and Mary when his telegram was delivered. They had been thinking about calling it a night before long, but changed their minds for the time being. They would remain in the Diehard until the Tumble train crew and passengers bound for Echo arrived with accounts of just what did happen.

They didn't have long to wait, for the Tumble engineer scorched the rails on the way to Echo.

Knowing where the sheriff would very likely be, the train crew and passengers with Echo their destination descended on the Diehard in a body, and the holiday got another boost.

"And I reckon you figure it was one of Messa's capers, eh? the sheriff remarked to Slade.

"Of course," the Ranger replied. "All the marks of his handiwork. Yes, he put one over nicely tonight."

"Then he's well heeled with *dinero*," said Crane. "The messenger told the Tumble conductor that there was a lot of money in his safe, consigned to the Sanderson bank."

154

"Well, thank goodness you two were not mixed up in it," said Mary. "I feel I have plenty to be thankful for this night. I want a glass of wine."

"Recompense for showing your boys a good time," the sheriff told her. "They figure tonight is just a warming up for their real holiday tomorrow."

"Hope I can bear up under the strain," Mary sighed.

"Oh, you'll make out," Crane predicted. "Yes, I think I'll have another snort. How about you, Walt?"

"I guess one more cup of coffee will help me sleep," Slade smiled.

After which, with another wild day in store, they called it a night, Lerner and Rice having already retired, the rancher with friends.

CHAPTER
TWENTY-TWO

Around mid morning, Slade arose greatly refreshed and in a complacent frame of mind. Messa had put one over, yes, but Slade felt he could hardly be asked to shoulder the blame for what happened. He could not be expected to be in several places at once.

That was the great advantage the outlaw enjoyed. He knew exactly what he was going to do, while the peace officer had to guess, and endeavor to grasp any opportunity that presented itself. And he believed he had done a pretty good job of grasping of late.

Well, it looked like he would put into effect something that had worked for him more than once in the past. Set a trap for the hellion. One he would walk into and wouldn't be able to slide out of.

He bathed and shaved and donned new clothes in honor of the holiday. Descending to the sitting room, he found the sheriff already there, puffing his pipe. The cook had insisted that they eat the breakfast he would prepare and never mind the Diehard.

Mary came bouncing down and seconded the cook's motion. Lerner had already eaten and was north of the breakthrough inspecting things there.

After they consumed their leisurely breakfast and pronounced it outstanding, the sheriff asked as he stuffed his pipe, "Now what?"

"Now I'm going down to the cart station and make sure everything is okay there," Mary said. "The boys should soon be starting their real holiday celebration."

"And I'll join Lerner at the breakthrough for a while," Slade said.

"See you both at the Diehard, a little later," said the sheriff.

Full fed and content, Slade strolled slowly through the cut, giving a once-over, and satisfied with what he saw.

The sides of the cut should not be neglected. A hard rain, or a sudden thaw after a hard freeze and talus would be loosened to roll down on the tracks. Could even cause a wreck did the fall take place with a train or an engine be passing through at the moment.

Negotiating the breakthrough, he came upon the busy scene beyond, where the big machine shop was being erected and the assembly yard laid out. Very satisfactory progress was being made on both projects. Jaggers Dunn was going to be pleased.

Slade watched the work for a while, talking with Lerner who had joined him. He beckoned Broderick, who was standing nearby.

"Cal," he said gesturing to the workers, "suppose you let them knock off at noon today, so they can give the carters a hand with their holiday. I've a notion they might like to."

157

"*Might* like it!" Broderick replied. "Talk about an understatement."

He moved to a group, relayed Slade's suggestion, chuckling delightedly.

A cheer went up. A voice bellowed, "Hurrah for the Old Man!"

Slade smiled and bowed to the high compliment.

Old Man has nothing to do with years of age. It is a title, an accolade bestowed by such hardy workers only on a boss they admire, respect and like. Some of those present were old enough to be his father, but to them Walt Slade would always be the Old Man!

More cheers as the workers began stacking away their tools, for it was nearly noon.

"And you've sure taken *them* in town," Lerner chuckled as he and Slade moved back down the cut.

They paused at Lerner's quarters to pick up the sheriff, then moseyed down to the cart station and the Diehard where the holiday was really beginning to make itself felt, and heard.

Mary joined them and they sat down at their table for a while to watch the antics of the carters.

"Rader is bringing out the dance floor girls and the orchestra who really don't come on until evening. I'll see to it that they will get a little bonus for their overtime work," Mary said.

Her companions nodded approval which the sheriff emphasized by ordering another snort; Lerner thought his example a good one. So did Slade, to the extent of a cup of coffee. Mary followed suit with a glass of wine.

158

"Look!" she exclaimed, "here come the girls. Aren't they pretty! Never mind, Mr. Slade," she added. "Keep your eyes in this direction."

Which Slade felt wasn't hard to do. She was by far the most attractive bit of fluff on the premises.

Or so he thought, and was willing to put it up for a vote, sanguine as to the outcome of the balloting.

However, the girls did not lack for partners. Which, Slade admitted, was as it should be. He relaxed comfortably, resolved to banish all cares from his mind and enjoy the fun. Lance Messa and his bunch could, figuratively speaking, go jump in the Rio Grande!

An excellent resolve. But there was one flaw in his reasoning. He was discounting his own tremendous vitality that forbade him being idle too long at a time.

So although he was thoroughly enjoying the exuberant hilarity on all sides, he was slowly getting restless. He craved action of one sort or another.

Under such conditions, walking in the fresh air always helped. And here the air was certainly not fresh, being about fifty-fifty tobacco smoke, and there wasn't much chance to do any walking.

He chuckled. Next he would be telling himself that a hunch was building up. Perhaps there was, but if so, it was still too vague to really justify that appellation.

Be all that as it was, the undeniable fact remained that he had to move around a bit.

Mary and Lerner were dancing. The sheriff was talking with Rader. With a quick glance around, he eased through the swinging doors and onto the busy street.

Yes, the streets were busy, but not packed like they will be later, and walking was a pleasure, the air not smoky.

For quite a while he wandered about aimlessly, gazing into windows, studying faces, listening to scraps of conversation his keen ears caught, but learned nothing he considered significant.

He walked to the edge of the oil field and stood gazing at the bristle of derricks. Monuments to "black gold" that for so many eons had lain quiescent at earth's heart, but now pouring forth its dark flood to further the restless ambitions of man.

Finally he turned his steps to the south breakthrough. From the south he would get a good view of the mountains before returning to the Diehard.

Walking even more slowly, he hugged the bristle of growth on the east side of the cut, to avoid the burning rays of the sun.

He had almost reached the south mouth of the cut when into it swerved a farm wagon piled high with produce. And an instant later, four horsemen bulged from the growth and made straight for the wagon.

The driver flung up a rifle, but before he could squeeze trigger a gun blazed and he toppled from the seat onto the sacks behind it to lie supine.

A white flame of wrath swept over Slade. It was plain murder!

Again the gun blazed and the bullet fanned the face of the swerving, ducking Ranger; the killers had seen him the same instant he spotted them. The gun blazed again. Another and another, and another sent the echoes flying.

160

But the advantage was with the man on the ground, an elusive target against the shadowy growth. Both Slade's Colts boomed, and again.

Two of the killers fell. Again those crashing twin reports, and a third rider spun from his saddle. The fourth whirled his horse and went racing out of the cut, the three riderless horses plunging after him.

Slade tried to line sights with the killer, but the wagon, the horses of which were moving, blocked him.

For a moment he stood with his eyes focused on the three motionless forms in the dust. Convinced they were satisfactorily done for, he holstered his Colts and sped to the wagon, climbed into it. The lumbering horses halted at a word.

A glance showed the driver bleeding from a scalp wound. The injury did not look too serious but needed attention without delay. Slade plucked up the fallen reins and sent the horses moving through the cut.

Evidently the shooting at the south mouth of the cut had not been heard, or had been disregarded as just part of the holiday celebration. He met nobody on the way through the cut.

It was different when he rolled the wagon through the streets to the Diehard. Yells, curses, questions stormed. The carters came boiling out of the saloon. Slade's voice lessened the tumult.

"Here!" he shouted as he halted the wagon. He passed the still unconscious driver to ready hands raised to receive him.

"Into the back room with him," he ordered and told the carters,

"Come up and unload this wagon and see what you find, especially under the grain sacks."

The carters scrambled into the wagon and farm produce flew in every direction. One uttered an exultant whoop as he hauled out a stout money poke, which he tossed to Slade.

The sheriff, Lerner and Mary had fought their way through the crowd. Slade passed the poke to Crane.

"Lock it up in Rader's safe," he said. "We'll check it later."

Now the wagon had been emptied. Meticulous search revealed no more pokes. Slade descended and hurried to the Diehard back room, Mary and the others following him. He found the wagon driver mumbling and muttering with returning consciousness. As he suspected, the injury was slight, just a lightly-creased scalp, the driver knocked out by shock. Slade quickly had the wound patched up. The driver had gotten his senses back and was staring about dazedly.

"Just take it easy," Slade told him. "Relax and drink the coffee they're bringing you. Don't try to talk for a while. Your money poke is safe."

The driver nodded gratefully and did as he was told.

"That's the Murchison General Store wagon," somebody volunteered.

"Somebody notify Murchison of what happened," Slade directed. "Tell *him* the money poke is safe despite that loco arrangement of sending it from Sanderson via the produce wagon, a perfect setup for the owlhoot bunch. Seems people will never learn, some of them."

"Walt," wailed the sheriff, "won't you please tell us what happened. And have you got any carcasses for me?"

"Send a cart to the south mouth of the cut to fetch in three," Slade replied. "One got away."

Crane gave a hollow groan and hurried to relay the order to Saxon. Slade patted Mary's shoulder and allowed her to lead him to their table, Lerner chuckling along behind.

Rader also accompanied them, after putting the wagon driver in the care of a couple of the floor men.

Slade gave them a brief account of what took place at the mouth of the cut. Mary sighed resignedly. The sheriff growled and muttered. Lerner and Rader seemed amused at the whole affair.

Slade knew there was nothing unusual in sending produce from Sanderson in a farm wagon, much the cheapest way to transport it. But the clumsy subterfuge of packing money under the produce had not been employed before. Slade felt it would not be again.

So, all in all, the holiday was a howling success, literally speaking. A number of railroaders having joined the carters in an endeavor to make it so.

Murchison arrived, highly agitated. He was quite subdued by the time the sheriff got through with him. He admitted there was a large sum of money in the poke, which was to expand his building.

"Who's doing the work on your building?" Slade asked.

"Lance Messa, the builder," Murchison replied. "He does excellent work."

"I see," Slade said dryly. He did, a number of things.

Murchison promised to take care of the wagon driver and the horses. Slade and his companions settled down to a snack and the appropriate side adjuncts. The holiday roared on.

"And you figure it was some of Messa's bunch tried to lift the Murchison poke, eh?" the sheriff remarked to Slade after the storekeeper had departed.

"Of course," Slade replied. "He learned about the money being hidden under grain sacks from Murchison, easy enough to do with Murchison trusting him as he does. Sent the four of his followers to handle the routine chore of killing the wagon driver and tying onto the money. Should have succeeded, one would say. Didn't appear to be any reason why it would not."

"Uh-huh, except *El Halcón*," the sheriff said.

"Rather, something utterly unforeseen," Slade pointed out. "By the merest chance I happened to be at the cut mouth when the wagon arrived. And my utterly unexpected presence threw the devils off balance, which they didn't recover soon enough. Otherwise the story might have had a different ending."

"Oh, you can always figure a way to keep from giving yourself credit due you!" snorted Crane. "Yes, everything would have been fine, from the owlhoot point of view, had not *El Halcón* tangled their twine for them. And you don't think the one that got away could have been Messa?"

Slade shook his head.

"I got enough of a look at him to be confident he was not," he said. "Not nearly big enough. No, Messa didn't consider it was necessary for him to take part in such a routine raid."

"Sure wish he had taken part," growled the sheriff. "Then right now we wouldn't be bothered about Messa. Oh, well, maybe next time."

"Let us drink!"

"And I want one more dance," said Mary.

The musicians and the girls, their bonuses tucked away, bowed and smiled as Slade and Mary moved onto the floor, which was not nearly so crowded. For it was getting late, and even the carters, with the long drive to Sanderson in the offing, were becoming subdued.

So, back at the table, Mary nodded to Saxon. With him in the lead, they trooped out, their faces ashine with pleasant memories. Undoubtedly the holiday had been a success.

Mary, Slade and the sheriff followed their example. Estevan waved from the kitchen. Peace and quiet descended on the Diehard.

CHAPTER
TWENTY-THREE

Everybody slept late, as was to be expected after the activity and excitement of the holiday bust, and there was no hurry to start the empties rolling to Sanderson.

Slade, Mary and the sheriff ate breakfast with Lerner, and took their time about it. Lerner and Mary made a final check of the loads requested, sent word to Slade and the sheriff that everything was set to go.

With Slade, Estevan, the sheriff and Deputy Blount accompanying them, the carts rolled a little past noon. The nice weather still persisted and it was pleasant riding across the sun golden rangeland. Birds sang in the thickets, the carters responded with song, or what was apparently intended for it. Slade and Estevan scouted ahead, per usual, although Slade felt fairly sure that the heavily guarded train was in little danger of being attacked. Just best not to take chances with that elusive and unexpected gentleman, Lance Messa.

The first line of breaks was negotiated without incident. The same applied to the second, third.

As they entered the fourth, Slade's vigilance increased, for here was the most dangerous stretch of all. Where the trail ran through the narrow gut closely flanked with tall stands of chaparral that would provide

166

cover for a score of outlaws, where one attempt had been made against the train. A futile attempt because of *El Halcón's* watchfulness. The gut, but a few score paces long, opened onto the treeless rangeland, where the train was in no danger.

As usual, even Slade breathed relief when the broad reaches of grasslands stretched on all sides.

With the dusk closing down, the lights of Sanderson were sighted, steadily brightening through the deepening gloom, and shortly afterward the carts were trundling through the streets of the railroad town. They were placed for loading, the horses cared for, and Slade and his companions assuaged their hunger in Hardrock Hogan's Branding Pen.

After eating, Mary went to her room in the Reagan House to rest a little. Estevan glided into the kitchen. Slade and the sheriff settled down comfortably with a snort, coffee, pipe and cigarette.

They were thus agreeably occupied when a young man whom Slade recognized as one of the bank clerks hurried in. He glanced about and made straight for the table.

"Mr. Slade," he said, "Mr. Charles, the president, would like to see you in his office, right away."

"Okay," Slade replied. The clerk hurried out. Slade rose to his feet.

"Get in touch with Estevan and Blount and have them make ready to move," he told the sheriff. "Looks like Charley may have hit on something."

Charley had. When Slade joined him in his office, he said, without preamble.

"Walt, something I figure you should know. One of those hush-hush deals was consummated in Tumble today. Dead secret stuff, of course, but you know what that means — secret except to those who most certainly shouldn't know about it. A man here is mixed up in the deal and a very large sum of money is being sent him, in a buckboard with a driver on the seat."

"Any idea when the buckboard should arrive?" Slade asked.

"From what I've been able to learn, I would say it will reach Sanderson, if it ever does, in not so much more than an hour."

Slade whistled under his breath. "If ever is right," he said. "Will be a miracle if it gets through the first line of breaks to the east of here. Okay, we'll do what we can."

"I'll be here when you get back," the president promised. "Good hunting!"

Slade returned to the sheriff at top speed. He found Deputy Blount with him, Estevan peeping from the kitchen.

El Halcón nodded and Estevan vanished. He had the greater distance to cover, but he would be at the stable first. He was getting the rig on his mustang when the others arrived there and cinched up at top speed. They led their horses out, mounted and rode east. Slade gradually increasing the pace until they were traveling at almost racing speed. He was forced to curb Shadow somewhat, in deference to the other cayuse's lesser ability.

"If a try is made for that money, and I feel sure there will be, it will be in the narrow gut close to this side of

168

the first breaks," he told the others, "where it will be simple to kill the driver of the buckboard, grab the money and escape in most any direction. Come what may, I figure it is showdown. We are taking a chance, riding across the open prairie this way, but we have no choice if we hope to save the driver's life. Doubtful if we can. I greatly fear we are too late."

The others muttered and swore, straining their ears to catch the sound of doom, a gun shot.

It came, loud and clear in the night air. Slade murmured bitterly. Crane and the deputy swore. Estevan caressed the haft of his blade.

Now they were no great distance from the mouth of the trail opening in the breaks, the horses speeding.

From the opening burst four riders. They instantly sighted the posse. Guns blazed, bullets whistled past. Slade shot with both hands, the posse guns boomed.

Two outlaws fell. Again those booming Colts, the crackle of the others' irons. A third killer went down to lie motionless beside his dead companions.

But the fourth, that Slade knew was tall Lance Messa, mounted on a fine roan, did not take time to fire but kept on going, south by west. And he had gained distance.

Slade drew his Winchester, settled himself in the saddle, and the race was on.

The roan was an excellent animal, but he wasn't Shadow. Soon he had given his all, and it wasn't enough. Shadow was slowly closing the distance between pursued and pursuer.

Slade saw the white blur of Messa's face as he turned to gaze back at the Ranger. Then the flash of his gun, the bullet coming close. Another just touched his cheek, still another twitched at his shirt sleeve. Another moment and his voice rang out,

"Surrender, Messa, or I'll kill you!"

He hoped to be able to spot his target, for he would have liked very much to take the outlaw leader alive.

Messa's answer was a scream of fury, and more shots. Slade threw the Winchester to the front, lined it, squeezed the trigger.

The big rifle thundered. Messa reeled back as if struck by a pile driver. He slumped sideways, toppled from his hull and thudded to the ground to lie supine.

With a regretful sigh, Slade rode ahead warily; but there was nothing more to fear from Lance Messa, able and adroit man who had not lacked courage. He was stone dead when Slade dismounted beside him.

The others came pounding, drawing rein as they neared the scene of blood.

"Got the sidewinder, eh?" the sheriff whooped. "I see the money poke is beside him. A clean sweep, just as it should be."

"But my blade it thirsts!" wailed Estevan. "Drink it did not."

Which provoked laughter, even though nobody was much in a mood for mirth.

"Load up the bodies while I locate the buckboard and the driver's body," Slade directed. The others got busy with the chore.

But when he neared the opening in the breaks, he got a pleasant surprise. The buckboard was just emerging from the opening, the driver on the seat, his face

170

streaked with blood that oozed from a head wound. He instantly recognized the Ranger.

"Mr. Slade!" he exclaimed. "Where in blazes did you come from?"

"Let me take a look at your head first," *El Halcón* replied. "Incidentally, your money poke is saved."

The driver sputtered his amazement.

A swift examination disclosed that his wound was not serious and could wait until they reached Sanderson for treatment.

The others of the posse, the bodies roped across the saddles, hove into view, to add their congratulations to the driver's.

"Thought you were a goner," said the sheriff. "Okay, let's head for town. I crave a snort."

There was plenty of excitement in Sanderson when the bodies were placed on the floor of the sheriff's office, the false beards stripped off and Lance Messa's face revealed. There would be even more excitement in Tumble and Echo.

Slade left the sheriff to answer the questions and repaired to the bank president's office, taking along the driver and the money poke. There he found Doc Cooper keeping Charley company.

"Figured he might be needed, so I sent for him," Charley explained.

The driver's injury was cared for, pronounced of little consequence.

"I'll hold an inquest on the carcasses tomorrow," Cooper, the coroner, said.

Present also was the owner of the money. It was passed to him, and he got a good scolding from the sheriff, who had dropped in at that moment. He promised to do better in the future. Which did not appear to impress Crane much.

Estevan had hurried to the Branding Pen to allay Mary's anxiety. After the horses were cared for, the posse joined her, to partake of a belated snack.

"And I suppose you will be hitting the trail now?" she said to Slade.

"Not for a week or so," the Ranger replied. "Mr. Dunn will be here most any day and I wish to consult with him, and say goodbye to Rice and others."

Something more than a week had passed when, as she stood stroking Shadow's glossy neck, she said,

"I'll be waiting, dear."

She watched him ride away, tall and graceful atop his great black horse, to where duty called and new adventure beckoned.

She smiled bravely, but her blue eyes were wistful.